GW00792363

Part Four
StoneSpell
by James David

Illustrated by Rex Aldred and James David

First Published in the United Kingdom in 2006
by Moonbeam Publishing

Copyright © James David 2006

ISBN No.13 978 0954 7704-33
ISBN No.10 0 9547704-3-9

Bibliographical Data Services
British Library Cataloguing-in-Publication Data
A catalogue record for this book is available
from the British Library

Printed and bound by:
The Max Design & Print Co
Kettlestring Lane, Clifton Moor,
York YO30 4XF

AQUA CRYSTA
- the first series

To my wife, Jo
for all her help and encouragement
in bringing the Magic beneath the Moors to life

AQUA CRYSTA

Part 4

StoneSpell

Chapter 1

The township of Galdo had known nothing like it! Never ever, during its long, long history, had there been such a celebration, such a festival!

Even the Coronation of Queen Venetia herself couldn't match it and that had been quite an occasion! Of course, that was many, many harvests ago, and although it was a splendid affair, its festive mood had been tainted by the tragic death of her husband, the good King Sigmund.

But now, the mood was pure joy and unbridled jubilation!

Everyone was in for the party of a life-time!

The towering Island of Galdo, sat proudly in the middle of Lake Serentina, was simply awash with colour, decorated to its very summit with fluttering festoons of petals and traditional triangular flags. Enormous garlands of flowers clung from every spiralling pathway, and lengthy ribbons of red, gold and silver dangled from every terrace. The island seemed alive, dripping with every possible colour under the Upper World sun!

As the *Goldcrest* glided across the mirror-like lake, heading for the quay, yet another excited boat load of Aqua Crystans from Pillo (the township at the other end of the Floss Cavern) felt their hearts beating faster and faster, as they approached the festivities.

They had heard about the happenings in Galdo, but this was more than they had ever expected in their wildest dreams!

The island looked magnificent...and this was only the outside!

What on earth could it be like inside?

Jonathan and Jane gazed in amazement at the wonderful sight before them as Captain Frumo guided the *Goldcrest* nearer and nearer to the small pier. Already, queues of eagerly chattering Pillonians had formed...each and every one of them, adults and children alike, anxious to disembark and step onto the magical island.

"Careful, everybody!" called the Captain from his wheel. "Make sure you queue evenly on each side of the ship, otherwise...well, I'll leave it to your imaginations!"

But he needn't have worried. There was no way that anybody was going to spoil the fun!

Instead, the usual, characteristic calmness of all Aqua Crystans prevailed, and the queues were orderly and even. Although, it must be said, that on this occasion, everyone on board was full to the brim with excitement... and they could hardly wait to spill over and really let their hair down!

Nearer and nearer, the golden vessel glided, her yellow sail billowing slightly in the warm breeze. The ship had left the current of the Floss behind and was now cutting across the placid water of the lake, her prow slicing through the odd raft of bubbly froth.

"Just look at that reflection!" beamed Jonathan, pointing over the rail at the perfect, watery image of Galdo, doubling its splendour.

His sister, her head resting on his shoulder, looked into the vast mirror. "It's beautiful!" she sighed. "I just wish Jessica and Jamie could be here to see it. I wonder what they're doing now!"

Strangely...(although perhaps not!)...the same thought had just crossed Jessica's mind as she leaned on the hand-rail of the small, wooden footbridge, gazing dreamily into the white, bubbling waters of the stream that burbled below.

"Looks like a bit of a climb ahead!" exclaimed her brother, as he clattered past her, shaking the bridge. "Race you to the top!"

"Just hold your horses, Jamie! There's no rush! We've got at least half an hour before dad arrives, and we've only one or two more clues to find!"

Jamie came to a sudden stop, made his usual car-skidding noise, and joined his older sister gazing down into the dazzling, narrow stream that flowed through the steep-sided Littlebeck Valley.

"I wonder what Jonathan and Jane are doing now?" said Jessica wistfully. "It seems ages and ages since we saw them last!"

"I bet they're both tucking into a couple of juicy, scrummy slices of roast chestnut, spread with yummy spoonfuls of bramble jelly with chunks of hazelnuts, topped with toadstool cream...and all washed down with that *dee...licious* oak-leaf tea!! And all that lot after having had a good lie in bed...as it's a Saturday morning!"

"Not *everybody* eats for a hobby like *you*, little brother!" Jessica smiled. "And, besides, it's never Saturday down there! Remember, there are *no*

days in *Aqua Crysta*! *No*
weeks, *no* months, *no*
years...*no time at all*, in fact!"
"Well, if they're not tucking
into breakfast, then I reckon
they're..."
Jamie paused for a moment to
watch a brown dipper fly from rock to rock, its patch of chest feathers
gleaming as dazzlingly white as the frothy water. They both watched its
comical jerky, bobbing movements after it perched on each rock, before
flying off downstream.
"I reckon," Jamie continued, "they're at this very second...wandering
round the market-stalls in the middle of Pillo..."
Jessica slowly shook her head, her long coppery hair brushing the
smooth handrail.
"...Or perhaps they're sailing down the Floss aboard the *Goldcrest*...
spray in their faces, watching the wonders of the Cavern glide by!"
sighed Jessica, lost in memories of her visits to Queen Venetia's magical
realm that lay secretly below the Upper World countryside.
"Or...I bet they're sitting on their balcony playing a game of *'Quintz'* or
'Sanctum'!" insisted Jamie, ruffling his mop of ginger hair.
"No...I can see them now...as clearly as the moss on that fallen tree over
there!" smiled Jessica, calmly and somehow knowingly. "I can see the
Goldcrest gliding across Lake Serentina and silently coming to a smooth
stop next to the small pier at Galdo. Yes, there they are! Jonathan and
Jane in a great queue of excited Aqua Crystans stretching all the way
round the deck! Already, the first passengers are stepping onto the
quayside! There seems to be some kind of celebration going on!
Galdo's decorated with all sorts of flowers and flags!
The island looks beautiful!!"
Jessica slowly raised her right arm and almost waved.
Jamie gazed at his sister and nudged her with his elbow.
"OK, OK, you win!" he said, mocking Jessica's powers of imagination.

4

"I suppose you're going to tell me next that Lepho's there, on the quayside, greeting everyone as they step ashore!"

"You're...absolutely...right!" said Jessica, still staring into the rushing waters of the stream. "Can you see the gold chain and medallion hanging from his shoulders? He's the *Mayor of Pillo* now! Remember?"

Jamie nodded, still going along with his sister's daydream.

"Is Queen Venetia with him?" he asked, sounding as though Jessica was reading the tea-leaves in the bottom of a tea-cup!

"No...I can't see *her*...but Lepho's holding...some kind of...small, wooden box shaped like a log with golden strips round it...and a sort of golden lock on the front! He's trying to shake everybody's hand and hang on to the box at the same time...and, he's peering anxiously at the queue on the *Goldcrest's* deck, as though he's looking for someone in particular..."

"...Jonathan and Jane, perhaps?" suggested Jamie, with more mocking tones in his voice, impatiently wanting to get on with their father's treasure trail through the woods.

"Alright, alright, I'm coming!" snapped Jessica, even more impatiently, and at last looking away from the stream's bubbly, enchanting spell. "But I'm *not* racing you to the top!"

As Jamie thankfully galloped up the steep, winding path that lead out of the wooded, flower-scented valley, Jessica followed slowly and glanced back at the babbling beck. The pictures in her mind had vanished, but she had felt strangely touched by their clarity and detail. It was almost as though she'd actually been there... by the quayside, as the *Goldcrest* had arrived at Galdo's pier! She knew she had a good imagination...but not *that* good!

This had been her best daydream ever!...but, like all dreams, it had lasted just seconds!

If only Jamie hadn't kept pestering!

She felt like going back to the little footbridge and staring into the water again, but already her brother was out of sight.

She stopped, closed her eyes tightly, and tried to see the quayside.

But it had gone.

Everything had gone...the *Goldcrest*, the queues of Aqua Crystans, Jonathan and Jane, Lepho, his gold chain and medallion, the wooden casket with the golden strips! Everything! The magic was over!

She opened her eyes and plodded up the narrow path sadly, as though she'd lost something precious.

"Come on, slow coach!" came Jamie's voice from round the bend. "I think I can see where the next clue is!"

Immediately, like a switch had suddenly clicked in her mind, Jessica jolted back into reality...picked up her speed, caught up with her brother and even jogged past him!

"Race *you* to the top!" she panted, laughing at the same time. "Who's a slow coach now?"

"No chance!" beamed Jamie, as he chased his sister along the path that wound upwards and out of the valley between huge, green-tinged boulders and tall, smooth-barked beech trees...the warm, mid-afternoon air full of the songs of chaffinches, greenfinches, bluetits, wrens, blackbirds and thrushes.

Suddenly, with no warning, just as she was about to be overtaken, Jessica slammed on her brakes, and pointed to the top of the path.

"Wowee!" she gasped, breathlessly. "Just look at *that!*"

And amazingly, at the very same time, on Galdo's small, wooden pier, Lepho greeted Jonathan and Jane and showed them the log casket.

"Wowee!" gasped Jane. "Just look at *that!*"

"It's amazing, a box made from a log cut in half!" burst Jonathan.

"And just look at those green gems embedded in the gold strips!"

"Where did it come from, Lepho?" asked Jane.

"That is exactly the first riddle we have to unravel!" replied Lepho, inspecting the casket closely. "I've been waiting to show you ever since Megan Magwitch presented it to me! I had to show Her Majesty first, you understand, but now, as the Queen said herself...we have a mystery solve!"

"But how come Megan Magwitch had it in the first place?" asked Jane, her red-ribboned pigtails bobbing around her shoulders.

"One of her daughters...Melita, I believe...found it washed up on the shore near *Torrent Lodge!*" replied Lepho, rubbing his ginger beard.

As the rest of the *Goldcrest*'s passengers jostled by, the three of them gazed at the strange box.

"What is the second riddle we have to unravel?" asked Jonathan, feeling the gleaming emeralds on the golden bands.

"Well, young man," explained the Mayor of Pillo quietly, his ginger eyebrows knitted together, quivering with curiosity, "it is clear the box is a box...but there seems no way of opening it to reveal its contents...that is, of course, if there are *any* contents at all!"

Jonathan and Jane felt all around the casket, and it was soon apparent that the short log was indeed split into two halves, but there seemed to be no way of prising them apart.

"It must be something to do with this golden clasp on the front," suggested Jane, her fingertips exploring its intricate design.

"Well, I have been attempting to encourage the casket to open since I have had it in my possession," sighed Lepho, "but so far I have had no success whatever!"

"I wonder why the log suddenly appeared in the *Cave of Torrents*?" asked Jonathan, excited at the thought of another mystery.

"But most of all, we have to find out how to open it and discover what's inside!" whispered Jane, her brown eyes growing bigger by the second. "But first, my friends," burst Lepho, tucking the casket away beneath his cloak with a flourish, "we have the pleasures of Galdo's Festival to enjoy! Come, let me show you the sights!!"

Jonathan and Jane followed Lepho as he wove through the crowds of excited Aqua Crystans. Most were flocking into the glowing red passageway which lead to the inside of the island. All the doorways along the tunnel were open with different exhibitions in each room, but each one was so packed with their heathery cloaked countryfolk that Jonathan and Jane just quickly peeped between the heads and shoulders on tiptoes and then pressed on into Galdo's magnificent interior.

As they approached the end of the tunnel, the noisy hubbub grew louder and louder, until suddenly, the whole wonderful, towering splendour of the inside of Galdo could be seen, dwarfing the river of visitors pouring into it. In normal times it was always a sight to behold, but now, for the Festival, it was absolutely fantastic!

The soaring, pink, circular walls of the inside of the vast stalagmite were alive with coloured flags and flowers draped from the spiralling pathways.

Galdonians who lived up in the island's lofty heights waved and cheered and threw armfuls of chopped petals down on to their delighted guests below. The air was full of the scents of Upper World Spring and early Summer...honeysuckle, May blossom and meadowsweet...all combined into a rich, heady perfume.

And, of course, this was partly what the Festival was all about... a celebration of all that could be harvested from the woodland above, especially from now until Wintumn when the first frosts would whiten and deaden the Harvestlands.

But for now, the whole of *Aqua Crysta* was in party mood with laughter and singing everywhere. So much so that Jonathan and Jane almost forgot about the wooden casket's treasures, as they gazed upwards into the criss-cross maze of aerial, hammocky walkways which looped across the towering space between Galdo's walls. Some even boasted amazingly daring displays of mid-air dancing with brave, colourfully dressed Aqua Crystans dangling from the swaying bridges on swings and grass-plaited ropes.

Everything was a wonderful treat for the visitors to feast their eyes and noses upon!

Suddenly, just as the trio wandered into the *Everlasting Toadstool Picnic Spot,* which lay more-or-less in the middle of Galdo's vast, circular floor, Jane's eye was caught by a glint of light from a market-stall...a stall just beyond one of the many blazing, crackling cooking-fires.

Indeed, the stall had already attracted quite a crowd of Aqua Crystans from their picnics! (An amazing feat in itself!)

Jane quickly grabbed hold of her brother's arm and pulled him over to the wonderful array of carved crystal that adorned the table. Lepho followed and the three of them looked admiringly at the crystal-carver's display.

"They're not all mine!" chuckled the small, almost dwarfish, white bearded man behind the stall. "Some of them are a couple of hundred harvests old! They'd be genuine antiques in the Upper World!"

There was everything you could imagine, all delicately carved from the pinkish and white crystal found throughout *Aqua Crysta.* There were crystal castles and towers, badgers and eagles, vases and candlesticks, and jewellery items to wear by the bucket full!

Lepho was enchanted by a crystal chess-set with pink and white glassy men ready for battle on a matching board of crystal-slice squares. Jonathan liked the carved Upper World birds, especially a dipper perched on a rock, but it was a rough, almost uncut chunk of pink crystal, about the size of a cricket ball, that had enticed Jane to the stall, mainly because of the way it glistened and shone.

It didn't have any particular shape, but on one of its sides was carved a narrow doorway...and strangely, on the top, were a pair of comfortable looking crystal armchairs...on the roof of what seemed to be a tiny, windowless house. She looked closely and found that, through the door, the chunk of crystal was completely hollow and rounded inside, making a single room. A horse-shoe shaped crystal bench ran around the bottom of the inside wall, broken only by the doorway.

"It's called '*The Hermitage*' !" said the man behind the stall with a grin. "Carved by old George Chubb who lives up in the third heights of Galdo. He came here from the Upper World in their year, *Seventeen Hundred and Ninety*! If you look closely you'll see his initials on the front...and the year he came here...and the name of the piece!"

But it was then, just as she was about to pick up the carving to have a closer look, that Jane suddenly noticed two tiny figures. Not crystal figures, but real, moving figures, just by the carved doorway, peering into the hollowed-out room.

She blinked and looked again, hardly able to believe her eyes!

And then, to her complete amazement she recognised them.

She knew exactly who they were!

The two figures dressed in pullovers and jeans, and wearing green wellington boots were unmistakable. A girl and a boy. The girl with long, smooth copper hair and the boy with a tangle of ruffled ginger hair. But they were so *tiny*...even smaller than the height of the carving's narrow doorway!

"*Look*! *Look*!" she suddenly exclaimed, pointing at the crystal and making Lepho, Jonathan and the little man behind the stall nearly jump out of their skins.

"Look, can you see who they are? Down there, by the doorway?"

The others looked, but they couldn't see a thing.

"Quickly, look, just there...before they go in...you must be able to see them!"

But they just shook their heads and looked at one another.

The other Aqua Crystans in the crowd around the stall looked equally puzzled.

"Jane, *what* are you talking about?" asked Jonathan, knowing that his sister wasn't normally into flights of fancy. "We can't see a thing! No one can see anything! It must be your imagination!"

"But I haven't got an imagination!" insisted Jane. "I tell you, I saw them...just there...looking into *The Hermitage*!"

"Exactly who did you see, young lady?" chuckled the little man behind the stall, beginning to feel a little sorry for Jane.

Jane looked first at Lepho...and then at her brother... and then, in a slightly shaky voice, she replied...

"Jessica and Jamie, of course!!!"

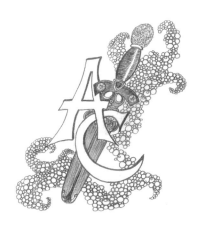

Chapter 2

Surely, it was the largest possible boulder that lay at the very top of the steep, winding path out of the valley!
But it wasn't its size that mesmerised Jessica and Jamie!
It was the amazing fact that the giant sandstone boulder had a *doorway* carved into one of its faces!

A doorway! Taller than Jessica and as wide as them both put together! How could a boulder have a doorway leading into it?
It seemed so strange! Jamie reached it first...and tentatively peered into the great rock's inner darkness.

"It's fantastic!" called Jamie, his voice echoing backwards and forwards across the empty, rounded insides of the huge boulder.

"It's been completely carved out to make a room!"

He turned to face Jessica who was standing nervously outside in the sunshine.

"Come into my parlour, said the spider to the fly!" beckoned Jamie, in as deep a tone as he could muster...his voice spookily magnified and deepened even more by the rocky cellar. "Fee-fi-fo-fum, I smell the blood of an English gir...!"

"Oh, shut up, you wimp!" laughed Jessica, as she suddenly plunged out of the warmth into the cool darkness.

Both of them sat down on the horse-shoe bench that wrapped around the bottom of the circular wall, broken only by the entrance.

"It must have taken years and years and years to hollow out!" said Jessica, as she gazed around the orangy, sandstone room. "You can see all the little marks in the rock where some sort of cutting tool has been struck by a hammer."

They felt the rough, jagged rock that surrounded them and spotted initials, names and dates that different visitors to the Littlebeck Valley had carved...*J.W. 1970...Bear '74...*

"Look, there's '*McD*'!" pointed Jamie with a grin. "Surely it couldn't be the work of Miss McDougal!"

"No, little brother, I'm sure it isn't!" smiled Jessica, remembering their teacher in the tiny village school, back in Scotland. "She used to tell us about her great hikes north of the border, but she never mentioned she'd been to Yorkshire!"

The room was almost perfectly round with a gritty, sandy floor and was about twice as high as Jamie.

"But, who could have hollowed it all out?" pondered Jessica, in admiration of the sheer perseverance and hard work of whoever had done it.

"Come on, let's explore the outside!" suggested Jamie. "Perhaps we'll find dad's clue!"

In next to no time, they were both looking at the neat letters and numbers precisely carved on the outside of the enormous boulder.

"What's a *hermitage*?" asked Jamie. "I've only heard of a *hermit crab*!"

"Well," started Jessica, "a hermit is someone who has decided to live all by himself away from other people in villages and towns, so I guess a hermitage is the place he has built to live in!"

"So this place is like a hermit crab's shell, then?" wondered Jamie. "And when the hermit guy got too big for this place, he sort of left it and found another hermitage!"

"Something like that!" smiled Jessica. "I suppose the hermit was 'G.C.', whoever he was!"

"Well, I reckon it's a pretty smart shell," admired Jamie, "and it's even got a balcony overlooking the treetops in the valley!"

True enough, with its base awash with brown, fallen leaves, was a half-circle of neatly cut rocks making a low wall. At each end was a long tall stone with a pointed top, like a small gate-post.

Beyond the wall was a superb, bird's eye view of the towering old trees in the valley and the winding silver stream further below. Across the tree-tops lay the distant moors where dad's treasure hunt had begun, earlier that morning.

Jessica and Jamie had always loved their father's treasure trails when they'd lived in Scotland...and this was the first that he had laid for them since they'd all arrived in Yorkshire the Summer before. As a rule, he usually hid about a dozen or so clues over a two or three mile ramble...each one leading to the next.

On this trail, Jessica and Jamie had already found ten clues...the last one being near the wooden footbridge in the bottom of the valley.

That one had told the children:-

"Beyond the bridge, a path so steep,
But at its top, just have a peep,
Atop a house cut out of rock,
Without a door for you to knock!
Under George Chubb's rooftop seat,
Is where my clue you shall meet!"

"George Chubb!" exclaimed Jamie. "That must be 'G.C.'! He must
have been the hermit...and look, there's something on top of the boulder!
It's like a rock armchair! That's the *'rooftop seat'*!"

A moment later they had both scrambled up a steep,
soily slope and climbed on to the roof of the hermitage. In fact, there
were *two* stone chairs...one larger than the other. Jamie, of course,
immediately plonked himself down in the bigger one and looked out
over his kingdom!
"I must say it's pretty comfortable," he laughed, "even though it's made
from solid rock! Makes me feel like *Fred Flintstone*! Hi, *Wilma*!"
"And, what a view!" marvelled Jessica, sitting in the smaller seat and
gazing over the lush, green tree-tops, as a flood of sunshine burst from
behind a heavy, grey cloud. "And to think that George Chubb sat here
over two centuries ago! I wonder if he liked his life as a hermit?"
Jamie felt under his throne, his fingers itching to find the next clue.
"Yes, it's here!" he exclaimed, producing the tightly folded green
paper...their father always used the same green paper for treasure trails.
He hurriedly unfolded it and quickly read it to himself.
"Come on, read it out, Jamie!" insisted Jessica. "The treasure's not just
for you!"
"Right then, here goes, and I reckon it's the last clue...

"Along the track marked Coast to Coast,
Come to a point that sees the most.
Deep below stands an ancient Hall,
By it, a tumbling waterfall.

There, find his Lordship by the gate,
Behind him, your treasures await!"

As the afternoon sun seemed to shine brighter and brighter in a gradually less cloudy sky, the children left the peculiar rock dwelling and made their way along a flattish path following a honeysuckle and ivy clad wall that looked over the valley. The wall petered out after a while to be replaced by a line of tall beech trees. Grey squirrels darted about everywhere searching for beech nuts amid the splendid splashes of bluebells. There were signpost reminders every so often telling them that the path was part of a much longer one that crossed England linking the North Sea with the Irish Sea...the '*Coast to Coast*' path in their dad's clue.

Moments later, the path narrowed and dipped above a steep drop into the valley below.

"There's the *ancient Hall* and the *waterfall*!" burst Jamie, grabbing hold of a wooden handrail. "You be careful!" warned Jessica. "That's quite a drop, and I'm certainly not going to climb down to rescue you!"

Soon they were standing in front of the old, deserted hall with the roaring, white curtain of water tumbling over a rock shelf next to it. "No wonder no one lives here!" shouted Jamie above the din. "They'd never get to sleep at night!"

But Jessica wasn't
listening.
She was already
miles away, staring
into the hypnotic,
pulsating waters that
plunged into the
churning, dazzling
froth below.
'It's just like the
great curtains of
water that
fall at each end of
the Floss Cavern in

Aqua Crysta,' she thought, as she felt herself being drawn once more
into the magical realm beneath their forest.

As the waters splashed and tumbled, pictures began to form before
her eyes...pictures so crystal clear and detailed that they sent shivers
dancing down her spine!

The images were of Galdo again, but this time they
were of the inside of the great, hollow stalagmite...its worn, smooth
crystal floor thronging with crowds of merry-makers mingling around
colourful and packed market-stalls and wandering between
the famous *Everlasting Toadstools*. She could almost smell the smoke
drifting from the nutshell fires of the popular picnic spot. Above them,
twisting and turning acrobats dangled from the maze of aerial walkways
that criss-crossed the island's towering, tapering heights. They were all
brightly dressed and looked like string puppets.

In the distance, just beyond the toadstools was the Queen's Palace...
and there...standing on its front door steps..!

But, suddenly, her daydream was cut short by a call from behind her.

"I've looked *everywhere* around the hall and I can't see any sign of a
'*Lordship*'!" Jamie complained. "What's dad on about?"

Jessica reluctantly looked away from the waterfall and gazed at the small, neat hall with its five windows and single doorway all blocked with concrete blocks and wooden boards.

It was solidly built of green-tinged sandstone with a red tiled roof held between a pair of squat, bookend chimney stacks. It certainly wasn't a ruin but looked as though it hadn't been lived in for years and years!

"I wonder who lived here?" called Jamie, above the roar of the water. "It's certainly a grander place than George Chubb's *'Hermitage'*...but where *is* this *Lordship* guy?"

"You keep searching!" called back Jessica, anxious to lose herself again in the torrenting water. "I'll come and help you in a minute!"

"If you don't, you're not getting any of the treasure!" replied Jamie, his freckly face showing signs of impatience with his sister.

To Jessica's relief he quickly dashed out of sight and explored behind the sad old building, while her eyes returned to gaze into the alluring white waters...

...and remarkably, as clear as crystal...on the steps of Queen Venetia's Palace...were...she rubbed her eyes in amazement, and looked again... yes, there they were...

...Jonathan...Jane...and Lepho....and then, as Jessica stared into the churning froth at the foot of the falls...the Queen herself appeared in the small doorway and greeted her visitors!

"I have been expecting you!" she said gracefully, with her golden hair cascading over her deep green gown. "I knew that as soon as you set eyes on the golden log casket you would want to discover its purpose and meaning! Come in, and we will talk more!"

And with that, the steps emptied as Jonathan, Jane and Lepho disappeared into the amazing crystal Palace...and so too, unknown to any of them...did Jessica!

It was just as she remembered from her visit the Summer before...the pure crystal walls, just like glass...the giant, shimmering, iridescent blue jay feathers creeping up the walls like plants and curling along the ceiling.

It was *all* there, but as an image in the tumbling waterfall, yet Jessica felt as though she was actually *inside* the Palace with her Aqua Crystan companions!

"I can't find him *anywhere*!" burst Jamie suddenly from behind her, again shattering the picture that only she could see.

The wonderful images just faded and dissolved like frost from a wintry window. Jessica was heartbroken, feeling again that she had lost something precious.

"Look around the gate like dad's clue said!" snapped Jessica, swishing her long hair back over her shoulders, as she always did when she was annoyed.

"You come and have a look!" Jamie replied sharply. "We'll never find the treasure before dad arrives to pick us up!"

"Just give me a minute!" Jessica called back over the roar. "I'm sure I can see something in the waterfall!"

"Oh no! Not again!" shouted Jamie, looking up to the sky and shaking his head. "That does it! If I find anything, it's all mine!"

"Alright! Alright! I give in! Just disappear!"

Jamie once again vanished around the back of the hall while Jessica, hurriedly and expectantly, returned her gaze to the torrent.

The question was...would the pictures return?

Or had they really been part of a daydream and the product of her vivid imagination?

She stared and stared at the rushing, splashing water, but nothing appeared.

Nothing at all.

The only thing that caught her eye was another bobbing dipper flitting from rock to rock in the large, rippled pool below the waterfall.

As she watched it, she was entranced by its low, jerky flight over the water...until, suddenly...it disappeared from view into the frothy, churning waters at the very foot of the fall!

She gazed intently at the spot where the bird had flown through the glistening, white curtain in the hope of seeing it re-appear.

She stared and stared for almost a full minute.

There was no sign at all of the dip...

...but then, all at once, at the very same spot the bird had flown through the frothing torrent...a figure, a very familiar figure...emerged, and slowly...looked up towards Jessica...

...and then, gracefully, raised an arm and beckoned to her...!!

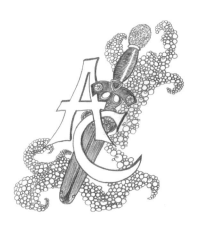

Chapter 3

The figure was Queen Venetia, and once again, Jessica could feel herself being magically drawn into her Palace. "You left us for a while!" said the Queen with a smile, as Jessica seemed to drift past her, through the doorway and back into the beautiful crystal room. She didn't know whether or not she could be seen by the Queen's other guests...Jonathan, Jane and Lepho...but she presumed not, as they chatted away and nibbled slices of meadow-sweet loaf dripping with creamy, yellow dandelion sauce.

As the Queen poured oak-leaf tea from her crystal teapot into matching teacups, she began to talk about the mysterious casket, which sat on her beautifully shining, hazelnut table.

"I believe that this curious arrival into our world is of some great significance," she began, "and I have reason to consider that our friends in the Upper World are involved in some way that is not yet clear."

"Excuse me for interrupting, Your Majesty!" burst Jane. "But I'm sure I saw Jessica and Jamie on one of the stalls at the market, here in Galdo!"

"Jane, for goodness sake, don't start going on about that again!" laughed Jonathan. "There was nothing there at all. I didn't see anything and neither did Lepho nor the old chap behind the stall!"

Lepho shook his head in agreement, but the Queen eyed Jane curiously.

"Strangely enough," she said slowly, "I, too, have seen Jessica...or rather, not *seen* her but *imagined* her...*here* in the Palace!"

She paused and looked at the much respected Mayor of Pillo.

"Lepho, I feel that we are in the midst of some kind of mystical...how shall I put it?...some kind of *mystical contact* between us and the Upper World! I feel whatever we say will be heard by our friends up there...or, perhaps, by Jessica alone!"

Lepho rubbed his stubby ginger beard and looked at his companions one by one.

"Although I cannot think of anything similar having ever been talked or written about in our long history, there is always room for unknown magic. Perhaps you are correct in what you say and that the discovery of the casket and the sightings by Jane and yourself are of no mere coincidental happenchance...but, are indeed, occurrences of great importance!"

"I agree!" said the Queen positively and with a certain amount of determination in her voice. "So I think we ought to discuss a plan with the view that our friend Jessica is somehow *here* with us, in spirit, if not in person!"

Lepho and Jane agreed and instinctively looked around the crystal room. Jonathan was more sceptical, but for the moment would say nothing. Nevertheless, he still rather anxiously looked around, as if he really wanted to see one of his Upper World friends.

Jessica, of course, and to her astonishment, could hear and see all that was happening in the Palace. It was all there, like a video being played in her mind while she leaned on the top rail of the wooden fence and gazed into the roaring waterfall next to the ancient hall! All she hoped was that her magical daydream wouldn't be suddenly shattered again by her brother. She *had* to hear the plan that was about to be hatched by the Queen and her guests!

But, as *you* will know from your own experiences of hopes...just when you want things to go smoothly...and however much you keep your fingers crossed....things go wrong, fate intervenes and hopes are ruined in a split second!

And, that was exactly what happened!

The pest in the green wellies!

"I've found it! I've found it!" came Jamie's excited yell from down by the hall.

In an instant the images of the inside of the Queen's Palace vanished and the brown and white dipper re-emerged from the churning waters at the foot of the waterfall and flew off downstream. Jessica was so annoyed that she could have cursed aloud or screamed at the top of her voice at her brother. But she knew *that* wouldn't gain anything! After all, Jamie would never understand her daydream nor take her seriously!

Best just to bite her lip and say nothing!

Reluctantly, she glanced a last look at the bottom of the falls and then trotted down to the two gate-posts that stood in front of the hall like a pair of miniature guardsman.

Jamie was feverishly examining the wall next to the gate-post with a broken top.

"Look!" he pointed out. "*Lordship* isn't a person, it's a *word*! Look here, it's carved in the rock!"

It was true.

In neat capital letters was the word '*LORDSHIP*' carved into the largest stone in the wall. The letters were half hidden by

moss and lichen, but in the bright sunshine they could easily
be read.
"And the clue said something about *'behind his Lordship'*, didn't it?"
said Jessica, at last, jolting herself back to the treasure trail.
She dashed between the gate-posts and saw a huge gap in the stones
directly behind the *Lordship* stone. Quickly, she delved her hand into
the damp, dark hole and excitedly felt for the treasure. It reminded
her of the day she and Jamie discovered the charms in the forest walls
the Summer before.
Suddenly her fingertips touched something hard and smooth!
Her fingers grasped the treasure and slowly drew whatever it was out
into the full glare of the afternoon sunshine.
They both looked at it with their mouths open wide with amazement!
Surely their father couldn't have hidden *this*!!!

        Already, Queen Venetia, Lepho, Jonathan and Jane had set
out upon their journey up the narrow, spiralling path which lead into
the heights of Galdo.
It had been decided in the plan of action to pay George Chubb a
visit in the hope that he may be able to help them. Perhaps he could
shed some light on the origins of the mysterious casket and why
Jane had seen tiny images of Jessica and Jamie standing
outside his crystal carved model of *The Hermitage* on the
market-stall.
                The pathway was one of the steepest in the whole
of *Aqua Crysta*, although not quite as steep as the steps up to the
Larder Caves from the River Floss. Nevertheless, the climb was very
tiring, and short rests had to be taken every so often. At each stop the
quartet were instantly surrounded by dozens of excited Aqua Crystans
all anxious to offer greetings and shake hands.
The pathway was lined with welcoming open doors, every house
hosting parties or entertainments from wine-tasting to juggling, from
painting to grass plaiting.

All sorts of performers and artists wanted to show off their skills, but the Queen and Lepho had to keep politely mentioning *'pressing business to see to'* and *'important meetings to attend'* as they climbed higher and higher into the heights.

Soon, looking down became a trifle uncomfortable, especially with the maze of swaying, hammocky walkways criss-crossing Galdo's deep, hollow interior. Together with the antics of the dangling acrobats and the heavy scent from flower garlands, all four began to feel slightly giddy and dizzy...and definitely anxious to reach the home of George Chubb.

"How far to go?" asked Jane, who was walking hand-in-hand with Lepho.

"We're almost there!" smiled the Mayor of Pillo, pointing ahead to a sudden widening of the pathway into a kind of terrace dotted with tables and chairs amid a sea of red and blue!

As they approached, they could make out two Aqua Crystans sitting at each of what must have been about twenty of the small circular tables. And, as tradition dictated, everyone was wearing a cloak of half of red and half of blue, instead of the usual heathery colour.

"It'll be the Finals of the *'Sanctum Tournament'*!" explained Lepho, gazing in admiration at all the intensely concentrating players. "I wish I could have entered myself, but the position of Mayor is too demanding on my time!"

Suddenly, a tall, rather angular looking man appeared from a doorway. He was grey haired and grey bearded, dressed in a long, ruby red robe and carrying a golden staff. As he turned to survey all the tables before him, he revealed the back of his robe...as expected, a deep, dark blue!

"George Chubb!" whispered Lepho to the others. "Crystal carver extraordinary, a man of unequalled skill, and *Sanctum Grand Master*!!"

At that moment, George Chubb's eyes met those of his distinguished visitors, and his face broke into an enormous grin.

"Your Majesty!" he exclaimed, in the deepest, most commanding voice you could imagine. "Your Honour, the Mayor...and *by, Jove*, the celebrated Jonathan and Jane!!"

Then his lengthy body bent into a most enormous bow!

Queen Venetia smiled and lead the others through the mass of tables. By now, all concentration among the players had vanished and everyone stood and welcomed the visitors. As she approached the still doubled-up Grand Master, he rather stiffly came out of his deep bow and offered his hand.

"We are greatly honoured by your visit, Your Majesty!" he announced. "Please come into my humble abode and refresh yourself! It must have been an exhausting journey!"

As the excited chattering subsided among the tables and the games continued, the visitors entered the small house cut into the Galdo's pink walls. Jane couldn't help pointing out its name carved expertly into its wooden door...'*The New Hermitage*'!

The inside of the lofty dwelling was absolutely magnificent, almost rivalling the Palace of Queen Venetia!

Both Lepho and the Queen had visited it before, several Harvests ago, but Jonathan and Jane had never seen such splendour. As they stepped through the small doorway, they gazed in astonishment at the beauty...all created by the hands of George Chubb himself!

The place was brimming over with the finest cut Aqua Crystan crystal of every shade of rose, from the most delicate pale pink to the deepest ruby

red. Shelves lined the room all packed with glistening, carved crystal images of everything possible from the Upper World. Every bird, every animal, every toadstool, even every flower head you could imagine, all cut into exquisite detail.

As well as the natural images there were dozens of chess sets on mirror-like crystal boards, vases and ornaments of every shape and size. And, of course, as you would expect, plenty of *Sanctum* sets with their delicately coloured crystal boards and characters. The chess set pieces were wonderfully carved but all just one tone or another of pink, white or red. But the *Sanctum* pieces had faces, clothing and hats! Jane was particularly taken with the *Fools* with their medieval minstrel checked suits and three-pointed hats tipped with gold bells. It was the *Warriors* which impressed Jonathan, with their fearsome horned Viking helmets, great shields and lethal looking broad-swords and axes!

But there was a group of carvings that entranced Jane the most. They were on a shelf in the far corner of the room, snugly surrounded by plumes of black and white magpie feathers creeping up the pink walls and curling across the glistening ceiling.

There was a model of a waterfall...its translucent, tumbling torrents frozen solid, like ice. Then there was a model of an arched, stone bridge spanning a rocky stream. But it was the carving which stood between those two that really captivated Jane.

It was of a house, rather like the dolls' house in the *Palace of Dancing Horses*...a house with five windows looking at her, a front door in a porch, and a pair of chimney stacks at each end of the roof. A low stone wall circled the building with a pair of pointed gate-posts opposite the porch.

"That's *Midge Hall!*" suddenly came the deep, friendly tones of George Chubb. "A wonderful building next to the waterfall and the stream with its stone bridge! I have fond memories of the place.

Before I came to live in *Aqua Crysta*, over two Upper World centuries ago, I used to visit it often to teach the children of the family, Josephine and Jasper...you know, the Josephine and Jasper who now live in Middle Floss. What a homestead it was! Full of beauty! The walls were covered with paintings and tapestries, and intricately carved wooden furniture filled the rooms. In fact, it was those chairs and tables that inspired me to carve...wood and stone in the Upper World, and then crystal here! I often wonder who has lived in the old hall since I came here. Indeed, is it still there? Or is it just a ru..?"

Suddenly, Jane grabbed hold of the old man's arm and pointed at the splendid crystal carving of the hall. She'd spotted something move just in front of the two gate-posts!
She blinked and looked once more.
"Your Majesty, I can see them again!" she called desperately. "Come and see for yourself!"
At once, The Queen, Lepho and Jonathan dashed over to the feathered corner of the room and all five stared in total disbelief at the sight before them!

Two tiny figures, dressed in pullovers and green wellingtons, were feverishly exploring every nook and cranny between the stones of Midge Hall's low wall, on either side of the gate-posts. This time, they were as clear as crystal to *everyone*!
"Jessica! Jamie! Can you hear me!" shouted Jane.
But before there was any chance of a reply, even more wonders began to

appear before the amazed, spellbound eyes gathered in the magical room way up in the heights of Galdo!

The crystal house was beginning to glow...brighter and brighter...as though it contained some kind of inner light!

Brighter and brighter!

So bright, the whole room was illuminated well beyond its normal pinky white!

Then, it became so dazzlingly brilliant that all five spectators just *had* to cover their eyes with their arms!

Next, there was a crackle...like burning, spitting wood on a fire!

Then another!

And another!

Silence followed.

Eyes, nervously and anxiously, peeped from behind cloaked arms and shaking fingers, and looked at the shelf.

Something was missing!

There was a gap between the crystal carvings of the stone bridge and the icy waterfall!

Midge Hall had vanished!

And with it, the two tiny figures!

But, at the very same moment, in the Upper World, under a bright Summer sun, Jessica and Jamie were staring, open-mouthed, at the treasure they'd found hidden behind the *Lordship* stone.

The glassy, crystal carving glinted in the sunshine.

Surely, their father couldn't have hidden *this*!!

Chapter 4

Jessica held the gleaming, rosy pink crystal carving and looked admiringly at its intricate detail - the windows, the two chimney stacks, the porch, the low wall and the gate-posts. "It's a model of this place, isn't it?" suggested Jamie. "The end of the treasure trail! It must have cost dad a fortune!"

Jessica raised her eyes from the treasure, looked intensely at the old hall behind her and then at her brother.

"This is nothing to do with dad," she whispered, as though hidden ears were listening. "Look at the crystal...it's from *Aqua Crysta*!... I'm sure it is!"

"But dad couldn't have...!"

Jessica suddenly stared over Jamie's shoulder into the distance.

"Look, look...on the stone bridge!"
she exclaimed, almost dropping the
precious carving.

For there,
walking serenely across the top of
the bridge, its tail pointing
skywards, as straight as a poker,
was a pure white cat!
"It's *Spook!*" burst Jamie. "From
Old Soulsyke last Summer!"
The sleek, graceful creature almost
glided to the middle of the bridge,
high above the rocky stream, and
then sat facing the children...its unforgettable, huge green eyes
twinkling in the sunlight.
"Jamie, hold on to me!" whispered Jessica. "We're in the middle
of some wonderful magic! What it's all about, I haven't a clue,
but..."
It was then that it began!
Spook's tail twitched from side to side...once, twice and a third time.
And before their very eyes, the two children were whisked into a
display of magic that was beyond their wildest dreams!

First, as they stood and stared, the fresh green
leaves of all the trees around the stone bridge turned yellow, then
orange and then brown! They'd withered and died, along with the
ferns and foxgloves of the forest floor! Summer had become
Autumn!
Months had flashed by in a matter of seconds as the children gazed at
the woodland before them!
And, all the while, Spook the cat, sat on the bridge and gazed back at
the children with its huge, green eyes.
But the magic wasn't over yet!
Spook's tail twitched again!

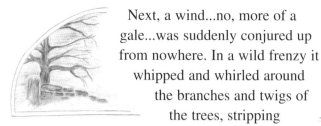

Next, a wind...no, more of a gale...was suddenly conjured up from nowhere. In a wild frenzy it whipped and whirled around the branches and twigs of the trees, stripping them of every single leaf. Almost instantly, the trees were bare and, as the gale retreated, the ground was carpeted in the russets and golds of October! But, miraculously, in a trice, all the fallen leaves were already tinged with glistening frost, as dense flurries of snowflakes swirled among the branches, clothing each and every bough in white!

Autumn had gone!

Winter had arrived!

And, still, Spook the cat sat on the bridge.

Its tail twitched again!

In moments, drifts of snow buried the fallen leaves, lapped nearby walls and covered the track. The gushing stream beneath the bridge seemed to instantly die and crackled into solid ice! In a flash...long, thin, pointed icicles grew downwards from the stone arch...but then, with equal speed, dissolved into nothing! The ice melted, the snow vanished, the stream swelled again...and buds appeared on the trees!

In a trice, the trees were green and everything was back where it started!

But, even then, the magic didn't stop!

As Jessica and Jamie gazed at the white cat, its tail twitched again... once, twice and then a third time!

Suddenly, a rumble could be heard of wheels on gravel.

Next, four dappled grey horses with silver manes appeared from the right-hand side of the stone bridge...and behind them a maroon and black stage-coach! It clattered over the bridge and stopped by a pathway.

Instantly, a small door opened and four passengers alighted...two adults and two children, all wearing the elegant clothing of Georgian England...the gentleman in a brown, knee-length coat with lace cuffs, deep pockets and wide lapels, all crowned with a golden silk cravat. Below the coat, his white stockinged calves lead to his shiny, black buckled shoes.

The lady wore a full, pale yellow dress which billowed wildly from her slender waist and swished and swept the ground, with dainty cuffs of lace at the wrists and neck. On her head was a prim matching hat adorned with extravagant feathers from far-off lands! She carried a folded, yellow parasol.

The children followed...a girl and a boy, no more than ten or eleven years of age. She was a miniature version of the lady except for the hat and the parasol...and he was wearing a white frilly shirt which tucked loosely into purple velvet breeches down to his knees. His buckled shoes were similar to the gentleman's and he carried a wooden hoop and a curved stick.

As the four-in-hand rumbled onwards and away along the track, they marched down the path, over a small wooden footbridge, and headed straight for Jessica and Jamie!

"Quick, behind the wall!" urged Jamie.

But, there was no need!

A moment later, the family had marched past them without even batting an eyelid...between the gate-posts and up to the front door.

Jessica and Jamie looked at one another in astonishment!

They seemed to be *invisible*!

They turned and stared, once again, in utter amazement!

Another miracle!

The Hall!!

It was *nothing* like it had been just seconds before!

The windows were lattices of shining panes of glass, behind which were large, fancy vases full of Summer flowers and framed by plush velvet curtains and lace. The stonework was fresh and almost orange, with not a hint of moss or lichen or rambling ivy!

Suddenly, the heavy, highly polished, dark wood door swung open and another, somewhat older gentleman appeared, dressed in a striped, mustard coloured waistcoat and trousers, a white shirt, a flowery bow-tie and scuffed, brown boots.

"Greetings, Lord Sneaton!" he said, with a smile and a bow. "I trust that yourself, Lady Sneaton and the children have journeyed well?"

"We have indeed, Mr Chubb, but Josephine and Jasper are anxious to return to your excavations at *The Hermitage*! Will you be able to entertain them this afternoon?"

"I will indeed," replied Mr Chubb, "but I have to say, my Lord, that my endeavours are almost complete!"

"I'm sure you can tire them somehow!" smiled Lady Sneaton. "The poor darlings are so restless after such a long journey from York!"

"While you work," suggested her husband, "perhaps you could enlighten them upon the fearful happenings which are occurring in France at the moment. The French are rebelling against King Lou..."

With that, the door closed, and the people from the late *Eighteenth Century* disappeared into the old Hall...and the completely confused and dumb-struck Jessica and Jamie, in their pullovers and green wellingtons, looked at one another with utter bewilderment!

What *was* going on?

They both turned, and slowly looked back towards the stone bridge.

Spook the cat had vanished!

And there instead...was their *father*!...sitting on the top of the bridge, his legs dangling down over the stone work!

"I see you found the treasure then!" he called. "Hope you like them... the squirrels haven't nicked the goodies, have they!"

Jessica looked down at what she had cradled in her hands.

Gone was the rosy pink, crystal carving of the old hall...and there, one in each hand...were two bright red, pottery mugs - one with '*Jessica*' printed in pink, and the other with '*Jamie*' in blue! And tucked in each mug was a little silver bag of golden chocolate coins!

Down in *Aqua Crysta*, at the very same moment, way up in the heights of Galdo...Jonathan, Jane, Lepho, George Chubb and Queen Venetia...once again shielded their eyes from the brilliant, bright light that filled the magical room.

They all heard the familiar sudden sounds that broke the silence.
A crackling...again, like burning, spitting wood on a fire.
Then another,
and another.
At last, curious eyes peeped from behind cloaked arms and shaky fingers, and everyone looked at the shelf in the feathered corner.
The crystal carving of Midge Hall had returned to its place between the icy waterfall and the stone bridge. Complete and unchanged, but with no sign at all of the tiny Jessica and Jamie.
The magic was complete, and its meaning was clear!
Some powerful force was at work!
Some *very* powerful force!
What exactly, was uncertain...
　　　...but what was in *no* doubt at all...
　　　Queen Venetia and Lepho *had* to do *something*!!

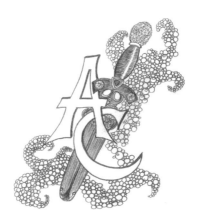

Chapter 5

"We've *got* to do *something*!!" whispered Jessica to Jamie, as they bumped along the narrow lane that lead from the small car-park, both of them nibbling chocolate coins.

They were sat on the back seat of the Land Rover, the front being taken up by three wooden crates full of potted larch saplings each wrapped in newspaper.

"Any chance of a spot of chocolate for the old man!" smiled Mr Dawson, glancing in the rear-view mirror, and turning his *Beatles'* tape down on the cassette-player. "What are you two whispering about anyway? It all sounds very hush-hush!"

"Oh, it's nothing, dad!" replied Jamie, leaning forward and feeding his father a disc of scrummy chocolate. "I just think that it's about time we laid out a treasure-trail for *you*, for a change!"

"Well, I'm certainly up for that!" mumbled Mr Dawson enthusiastically, with his mouth full. "Your grandad used to set them up for me, when *I* was a kid. I guess that's where the idea came from. Do you remember the ones we used to do in Scotland?"

Jessica and Jamie nodded, suddenly distracted from the amazing events of the afternoon.

"Especially the one that took us down the little glen to the loch!" beamed Jamie. "It was about twenty clues long! It took us all day to find the treasure by the little boat-house! I've still got that treasure somewhere...a couple of plastic dinosaurs, I seem to remember!"

"That's right, son!" laughed Mr Dawson. "I think they were supposed to be *Loch Ness Monsters*! Do you remember, Jess?"

She silently nodded.

Already, Jessica was lost in the depths of *Aqua Crysta*.

She just *knew* that she had to travel once more to the fabulous kingdom beneath the Moors!

The Magic was calling her...of that, there was no doubt!

"Are we heading back to *Deer Leap*?" she mumbled, as she gazed into the blur of yellow gorse by the road.

"We are!" replied her father, glancing at the crates of saplings.

"But first, I've got to drop this lot off at Bill Larkin's place!"

"Ace!" exclaimed Jamie, slipping the gold foil off yet another chocolate Spanish ducat! "That means we can pretend we're on the moon again! His farm's in the middle of a crater!"

"'*The Hole of Horcum*', to be precise!" laughed Mr Dawson, as the Land Rover began to climb up onto the moorland road that linked Whitby and Pickering. "But I know what you mean! It's a fantastic spot!"

Just ten minutes later, Mr Dawson drew into the car-park that overlooked the vast depression in the landscape.

"It takes my breath away every time I see it!" he gasped. "Come on, let's cross the road and stand on the edge!"

A moment later, the three of them were gazing into the depths of the enormous crater, the fresh breeze fingering their clothes and hair.

Down below was a patchwork of fields, stitched together by the hairline threads of winding footpaths and walls. Nestled amongst them were the stone buildings that made Bill Larkin's farmstead. They looked so tiny and distant. It was like looking down from a low flying aircraft, or floating in mid-air, dangling from a parachute!

"I wonder if it *is* a crater?" Jamie considered. "Perhaps a meteorite from outer space crashed here millions of years ago!"

"No, son! Geologists reckon that it was carved out by moving glaciers in the last Ice Age and then by lots of streams when the ice finally melted!"

"You mean, once-upon-a-time, Yorkshire was covered with ice?" burst Jamie.

"It sure was! Along with most of the rest of Britain!" explained Mr Dawson. "Ice, thousands of feet thick, so heavy that it carved away at the hills and mountains as it crept over the land, making deep valleys and flat plains all over the place!"

Jessica stared up into the sky, imagining great walls of ice towering above her. Then, as a burbling curlew flew by, with its long curved beak, she returned her gaze into the huge soup bowl below.

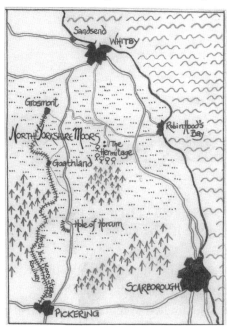

Tiny sheep and even tinier lambs were dotted about the green fields like stars in the night sky. The fields covered the floor of the basin, lapping up its steep sides and dissolving into the heather and bracken which climbed to the opposite rim at least half a mile away. Beyond lay the distant horizons of neverending moorland, still lacking the purple bloom that was to come in July and August.

"It's as though a giant came along and scooped up a great handful of earth!" smiled Jessica, imagining a gigantic figure astride the huge hollow, his boots the size of ocean liners, his legs like a pair of skyscrapers...his head and shoulders, way, way above in the deep blue, festooned with wispy strands of cloud. She could see him reaching down, blotting out the sun, and his great hands, the size of football stadiums, shovelling out great mountains of earth.

"Funny you should say that, Jess!" said Mr Dawson. "Legend has it that a giant did *exactly* that...hundreds of years ago! I think the giant was called *Horcum*...and that's why it's called the *Hole of Horcum!*"

"Perhaps he was another hermit...like that George Chubb bloke who hollowed out *The Hermitage* on the treasure trail!" suggested Jessica.

"But just a wee bit bigger though!" laughed Jamie, imagining his own giant curled up asleep in the gigantic hole. "Come on, folks, let's get down to Bill Larkin's place, then we can get back to *Deer Leap!*"

"What's the rush, son?" said Mr Dawson. "It's *Saturday*! We've got the *whole* day to ourselves...and it's just about the *longest* day of the year!"

"Of course, it's *Midsummer Eve* today, isn't it?" beamed Jessica. "Miss Penny was telling us about it yesterday at school! Tonight is the shortest night of the year and tomorrow is *Midsummer Day*, the longest day!"

"And Miss Penny said..." smiled Jamie, with a glance at his sister, "...that, tonight, *Midsummer Night*...has always been a night full of magic and mystery...when wizards and witches, fairies and demons all come out to make mayhem and mischief!"

"Yep! You're dead right!" agreed Mr Dawson. "And you know what? I'll be setting the alarm tonight for *quarter to four* tomorrow morning!"

"You're hoping to catch sight of a wizard or a witch, or something?" asked Jamie, with a gleam in his eye and another knowing glance at his sister...both of them secretly thinking about their own encounter with Merlyn, just a few weeks before!

Mr Dawson shook his head.

"Chance'd be a fine thing!" he laughed, totally unaware of his children's magical adventures. "No, it's the live telly coverage of tomorrow morning's sunrise at *Stonehenge*! Thousands flock there every year to watch it...and this year they're going to transmit the pictures all over the World! There'll be millions watchin'! I just hope it's not cloudy!"

At the word *'Stonehenge'*, Jessica and Jamie looked at one another again, this time a little more intensely. Each knew exactly what the other was thinking! *Stonehenge*...one of the three places in England where *Crystals of Eternity* had landed from the depths of space back in the mists of time...*Stonehenge* in Wiltshire, *Tintagel Castle* on the Cornish coast and near *Whitby Abbey* in Yorkshire.
They both vividly remembered how Jessica had helped Merlyn renew the power of the *Crystal of Eternity*, the magnificent, fiery stone responsible for *Aqua Crysta's* special magic!
It had all happened on Jamie's birthday, when Jessica had read aloud the words on Grizelda's gold medallion. The words unlocked the spell that had trapped Merlyn the Wizard in the guise of an Eagle Owl for centuries! Then, at the small lake near *Old Soulsyke*, they had watched the renewal of the *Crystal's* powers...and Jessica had received Merlyn's bejewelled dagger, *Verax,* as a reward!

As memories flooded Jessica's mind, once again she thought of the happenings of the warm afternoon. The pictures she'd seen of the *Goldcrest* arriving at Galdo, Lepho meeting Jonathan and Jane, the mysterious wooden casket, Queen Venetia beckoning her into her Palace...then Spook appearing on the bridge at the old hall, the amazing journey through the seasons, the crystal carving in her hands and the family arriving by stagecoach...

All seemed blurred, unclear, puzzling...but one thing was absolutely certain. She *had* to travel to *Aqua Crysta*...and the sooner the better!

Meanwhile, back in the heights of Galdo, as George Chubb's guests sat around a table sipping blue forget-me-not cordial from beautifully carved crystal goblets, Lepho suddenly remembered one of the reasons for the exhausting climb.
"Can you shed any light on *this*, my friend?" he burst, as he delved into his bulky grass-plaited bag.

A moment later, the log casket with the gold strips sat in the middle of the table, looking slightly out of place amid all the crystal.

"Well, well, well!" said George Chubb, with a look of fond recognition mixed with sadness written across his face. "That *does* take me back! But to see it again gives me a heavy heart."

"You've seen it before?" exclaimed Lepho, glancing at Queen Venetia.

"I certainly have!" replied the crystal-carver. "But I

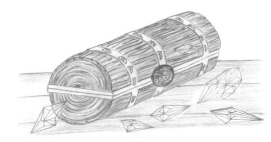

have to confess that when I laid eyes on it last, it was not embellished with golden bands! Its two halves were held together with rope!"

"When *did* you last see it?" asked Jane.

Mr Chubb gazed into the crystal clustered ceiling of his room, searching his memory.

Then he reached forward and his long fingers gently picked up the casket.

He drew it lovingly to his chest, as though embracing a long lost friend.

"This...," he began, "is the very last carving that Jasper completed in the Upper World before the three of us came to live in *Aqua Crysta*...back in the year *Seventeen Hundred and Ninety*!"

He paused and stared at the wooden box, reliving the past...over two centuries ago!

"We had just finished hollowing out *The Hermitage* in the woods overlooking the Littlebeck Valley. It had taken us nearly four Upper World years! The children were so proud of the work they'd done! They were only six or seven when they'd started helping me. I can see them now sitting on the thrones they'd carved on the roof. It had taken them the whole Summer of *Seventeen-Ninety* to carve them!"

He paused again and sadness suddenly swept over his face.

"It was the day that I'd carved the year above the doorway, a week or so after they'd returned from York with their mother and father, Lord and

Lady Sneaton. All the talk was of George Washington, who had just become the first President of the United States and Captain Bligh who had miraculously turned up after mutineers on his ship, *The Bounty*, had cast him adrift in the middle of the Pacific.

But I remember *that* afternoon we had been talking about the revolutionary troubles in France and how the people there were determined to rid themselves of King Louis and declare a Republic!"

Once again, the old crystal-carver stopped and his eyes welled with tears. "It had been a beautiful Summer's day. We were walking happily through the woods back to Midge Hall, humming tunes by Mozart, the maestro of Saltsburg, as we often did...when suddenly...we smelt burning in the air...then we saw smoke above the tree-tops...we started running...!"

Queen Venetia put an arm around the old man's shoulders.

Mr Chubb's voice deepened even more, and anger replaced sadness across his face.

"Then, as the waterfall and the hall came into view...we saw it!" he exclaimed bitterly. " The fire!! Flames pouring from every window! Thick, black smoke billowing into the sky! We stood and stared. There was nothing we could have done. But the worst was yet to come!"

He paused again, stood up from the table, slowly wandered over to the feathered corner and gazed at the crystal model of the old hall on the shelf.

"It was poor, young Josephine who noticed them first!" he began again, as his listeners watched him intently, dreading what was coming next. "Her piercing scream still haunts me! It echoed around and around the valley, even drowning the roar of the waterfall! I took her hand, but she desperately pulled herself free and flew down the path like the wind...screaming, screaming, screaming all the way!

'*Stop! Stop!*' I shouted after her. '*The flames! The flames!*'

But there was no stopping her! Jasper looked up at me. He'd seen them, too...lying there on the ground, motionless. His eyes were so full of sorrow and heartache.

I can see them now, pleading for an answer, an explanation.

He grasped my hand and we followed his sister...she, by now, was agonisingly hugging her dead mother, willing her to stir and hug her back...but she lay still and lifeless by the gate in front of the hall, next to the body of Lord Sneaton. And to add horror upon horror, tragedy upon tragedy...it was *not* the fire that had claimed their lives...they had both been *shot!*"

His stunned audience gasped.

"But *that* was not the end of it!" burst the crystal-carver, striding back to the table. "At the very moment we reached the bodies, we heard the sound of horses clattering over the bridge and down the path to the hall. Six, seven, eight of them, each mounted by fearsome riders yelling and wildly brandishing their firearms. *'Glory to the French Revolution!'* their leader called. *'Death to English nobility, one and all!'* The murderers were back! They were after the children!"

"But what did you do?" exclaimed Jane.

"We ran! We had to! There was no other escape! I dragged both sobbing, heartbroken children around the corner of the hall, across the rear courtyard and into the stables. A moment later, we'd cleared the straw in the far corner, opened the secret trapdoor in the floor and vanished into the *well-cellar,* as we called it...there was an open well shaft in one corner that lead down to a stream that never dried up, even in the hottest of Summers!"

Mr Chubb sat down, almost exhausted by his memories. He topped up the goblets of his dumbstruck listeners with more forget-me-not cordial and then carried on with his story.

"We huddled together in the dark and hoped and prayed that we wouldn't be discovered! We heard noises for a while, but soon all became silent except for the muffled roar of the waterfall from above and the rush of water from the well below. At last we lit candles and welcomed the light. Josephine and Jasper had often visited the cellar and enjoyed it as a secret hiding place, but on that day they were deeply distraught, as you can imagine. Tears flowed. They were inconsolable." The old man once again picked up the casket, turned it upside down and a long, shaking finger pointed to the faded, time-worn words... *'from Jasper'*...carved in small, neat knife cuts. Beneath them was the year *'1790'*.

"It was for his father," he said quietly. "He was making a surprise gift...a box made from a split log, hollowed out inside, the halves held together by knotted rope...and secretly made in the *well-cellar* under the stables. I remember, just after we'd lit the candles, the lad clutched the casket to his chest and burst into floods of tears. Then, in desperation, gripped by anger and rage, he ran over to the well and threw the precious gift down the shaft...a moment later we heard it plunge into the stream...and it was gone!"

George wiped tears from his eyes.

"*That* was the last time I saw it!"

The old man stood up and looked into each pair of moist eyes around the table.

"And *that* was the moment the magic began!" he whispered, with just the slightest hint of a smile returning to his lips. "For it was *then*...just after the casket was washed away...that we all heard the sound of a horn...a single, long, haunting note coming from the depths of the well shaft...and the rest, as they say, I believe...is *history*!!"

"Surely you couldn't get to *Aqua Crysta* by climbing down *that* well?" asked Jonathan curiously.

"No," smiled Mr Chubb, "we came here by way of the well at *Old Soulsyke*...but that's another story. I'm sure Josephine and Jasper will tell you that story sometime, if it's not too painful for them to recall. But tell me, Lepho...how do you come to have possession of the casket?"

The Mayor of Pillo told George Chubb of its discovery in the waters of the *Cave of Torrents*. Everyone then decided that, by some mysterious means, the stream under Midge Hall stables must run into the stream that flows past Torrent Lodge!

"The log casket has floated down both," concluded Lepho, "but has taken more than two Upper World centuries to do so!"

"And who has changed its appearance on the way?" wondered Jane. "Who has added the golden bands and the golden clasp?"

"And, above all, what is inside the box?" asked Jonathan. "And who put it there? We are still no nearer to an answer!"

They all fell silent and stared at the casket on the table, surrounded by empty crystal goblets. It was, indeed, a mystery to everyone...but one thing was certain...they now knew of its sad and tragic origins.

Together with the strange sightings of Jessica and Jamie near the crystal models of *The Hermitage* and Midge Hall and the latter's amazing disappearance and return...they were all convinced that powerful, magical forces were at work!

The question was...*what to do next*?

And *that* was exactly the same question that Jessica was asking herself, as she anxiously stood on the landing by her bedroom door, back at *Deer Leap*.

After the creak of the third step from the top of the stairs...another noise had made her suddenly stop...and listen!

It was coming from inside her bedroom!

A scratching, scraping sound!

Then a buzzing sound!

And more scratching and scraping!

Then a sharp crack!

Some*thing* or some*one* was in there!

On tip-toes, she inched towards the door, her heart beating faster and faster!

Her hand trembled as she gripped the brass door-knob, and slowly turned it...

Chapter 6

As silently as she could, she pushed gently on the door and put her face to the long crack of light. She could just make out her flowery duvet on her bed and the hedgerow wallpaper beyond.

She pushed again and the crack widened.

Her bedside drawers came into view...her reading-lamp...the pink rug and her furry slippers.

Everything seemed quite normal.

Then she heard the cracking sound again...and a scratch...and a scrape...and then a sudden burst of high-pitched buzzing, like a wasp in an empty coke-can!

She pushed again on the door, this time so that the crack became a gap, and was wide enough to put her head through.

Slowly, she peered around the edge of the door, her eyes becoming larger by the second!

Then...she saw it!

Under the window!

Something that didn't belong there!

Something she'd never even seen before!

Just then...another volley of noises came from somewhere near her bed! Instantly, her eyes darted from beneath her window to her bedside drawers.

What she saw made her mouth gape open in astonishment!

The dangling, pink fringe around her reading-lamp shade seemed to be trembling...shaking! All by itself! Like you imagine happening when there's an earthquake!

Suddenly, Jamie's voice from the bottom of the stairs rang in her ears!

"Are you ready yet, Jess? You said you wanted to get going as...!"

Quickly, his voice faded as Jessica, not taking her eyes off the lamp, wildly waved her arm and beckoned him to join her.

Jamie bounded up the stairs, three steps at a time.

"What's up!" he gasped.

Jessica, for a second, turned and put a finger to her lips. "Sssh!"

Then she pointed through the gap in the doorway and Jamie squeezed in front of her.

"Wowee!" he whispered. "What the heck is happ...?"

"I thought you two were going to set this 'ere *treasure trail* for me?"

Jessica and Jamie nearly jumped out of their skins!

It was their father at the bottom of the stairs!

"Why are you both standing outside Jessie's room, anyway?" he laughed. "Is there a ghost in there or something?"

"We'll be down in sec, dad!" smiled Jessica, a touch nervously.

"We're...we're...er, just going to find some treasure to hide for you!" stuttered Jamie. "*So don't* come up! It's *top secret!*"

With that, they both took a deep breath, pushed on the door and nearly fell into the bedroom! When Jessica had steadied herself, she tip-toed over to the drawers and lightly touched her reading-lamp. It had stopped shaking.

At the same time, Jamie crept over to the amazing pile of glittering, white dust that was on the carpet under the window...like a miniature pyramid of rock salt about as high and wide as one of Jessica's slippers.

Suddenly, another sharp crack exploded from the drawers...the loudest yet...like a plastic ruler being snapped!

Then came more high-pitched buzzing!

The reading-lamp fringe trembled again...and so did Jessica!

"It's coming from the top drawer!" she whispered.

Her hand slowly moved from the lamp and hovered above the drawer's handle.

"Shall I open it?" she whispered.

"We've *got* to!" replied Jamie.

"What do you mean? '*We've* got to'?" whispered Jessica, drawing back her hand. "You're well out of it, over there! *Anything* could happen!"

"Sis! It's a drawer, not an unexploded bomb! I've got my own mystery to solve!"

"Just come over here!" insisted Jessica. "We'll open it *together*...just in case! It could be something to do with the crystalid eggs!"

Jamie left his peculiar, white mound on the carpet and joined his sister by her bed.

They stood together, anxiously looking down at the top drawer.

"After three!" he whispered, a touch shakily. "You open it...and I'll grab hold of whatever's in there! Are you ready?"

Jessica nodded.

She moved her hand.

Once again, it nervously hovered above the drawer's handle.

"*One*...!" ventured Jamie, hesitantly.

They glanced at one another, their hearts throbbing.

"*Two*...!"

Jamie paused as Jessica took hold of the handle.

They both swallowed hard.

"*Three*!!"

Jessica pulled the drawer open...and instantly they were both nearly blinded by the sudden stream of brilliant bluish-green light that gushed into the room! They both instinctively shielded their eyes...but curiosity forced them to painfully look down into the drawer!

Through squinted eyes, the sight they saw made them gasp in wonder! Jessica had guessed correctly!

The crystalid eggs had somehow grown from the size of finger-nails to the size of fat sausages! And not only that...each of the five beautifully iridescent crystal tubes had shattered, broken open...and struggling out of each was a huge, chubby, squirming, brightly glowing grub like a giant fluorescent green caterpillar!

The sight of them crawling over the fossils and shells, pens and pencils in Jessica's bedside drawer made her blood run cold.

They were absolutely disgusting!

Strings of brightly glowing slime oozed from them as they scraped their crystal scaled bodies over one another, crunching and crackling the remains of the egg shells. At one end of each grub was some kind of mouth, and already they were devouring the crystal wreckage of their former homes. One was even gnawing at the green crystals Jessica had brought back from the Gargoyles' time-tunnel!

Then another's head rose into the air, swaying from side to side, as though sensing the air...impatiently waiting for its mother crystalid to fetch more food, like a fledgling chick in a bird's nest.

As Jessica and Jamie stared at these totally unknown, squirming creatures that had suddenly inhabited a drawer in the Upper World, they gradually became aware of what was happening in the rest of the dazzlingly lit bedroom!

Criss-crossing the walls, the ceiling, the floor...everywhere...were great, long streaks of sparkling, shimmering, multi-coloured crystal dust!

It was as though someone had wildly spread glue all over the surfaces with huge, swishing brush strokes...and then scattered sackfuls of glistening glitter!

The streaks were thick and thin, snaking and swirling over and under Jessica's bed, weaving and winding up the curtains, across the window, over the carpet...twisting and spiralling across the ceiling.

Some were even suspended in mid-air, looping from corner to corner, but they were solid and unmoving, not loose and saggy.

And somehow...every single one of the wild, frenzied streaks lead back to one place...the small pyramid of crystal on the carpet under the window, which was now almost pulsating with every colour under the sun!

But the strangest thing of all about them was the fact that they could only be seen when Jessica had opened the drawer!

Somehow, by means completely beyond the understanding of Jessica and Jamie, the sweeping festoons of crystal dust were only visible in the brilliant light cast by the giant, gruesome grubs!

But *who* or *what* could have created it all? And *why*?

Only a few hours before, Jessica had left her bedroom to go on her father's treasure trail. Everything had seemed quite normal!

But now her little bedside drawer was crawling with enormous caterpillars and the whole room was awash with mysterious, manic art-work!

Jamie reached up and touched one of the thick, drooping ribbons with his fingertips. It was about as wide as a scarf, but quite solid and cold. It was encrusted with crystals of all shapes and colours, running in streaky stripes along its length.

Neither of the children could even begin to understand it all, and as they were wondering what on earth to do next, things began to happen in the top drawer!

The grubs were beginning to crystallise!

Before their stunned eyes, the five chunky caterpillars had become perfectly still, and their fluorescent skins were hardening into solid crystal. It was like watching ice forming, but at a break-neck speed!

At the same time, their brilliant light began to dim...and with it the maze of crystal streaks began to fade and dissolve into thin air!

Moments later, the light had completely gone and the mysterious art-work in the room had vanished!

All that remained in the drawer were five iridescent, smooth, glassy tubes, still about the size of fat sausages! And all that remained of the streaks was their apparent source...the small, white pyramid under the window!

The children looked at one another, astonished by what they had witnessed. They sat down on the edge of Jessica's bed.

"I reckon the little crystalid eggs we brought back at Christmas have somehow grown and developed into the grub stage, and then changed into cocoons at the speed of light!" suggested Jessica. "The thing is...it might happen again...!"

"So we've got to take them when we go to *Aqua Crysta!*" laughed Jamie. "We can't leave them when dad's here alone! They could frighten him to death!"

"But the scarier thing is...!" said Jessica in a more serious tone. "Are you ready for this, little brother?"

Jamie nodded and tried to look as bold as possible, suddenly swishing his imaginary sword.

"Some*thing*..." Jessica began, dropping her voice to a whisper and gazing around the room, "...or some*one* has been in here while we've been out!"

"Wow...eee!" gasped Jamie. "Then we've definitely got to get going! In fact, I'm not staying here a minute lon...!"

He suddenly stopped.

"Hang on, sis! How do you know?"

"How do I know what?" replied Jessica in a weaker, more shaky voice.

"How do you *know* that some*thing* or some*one* has *been here*?" Jamie demanded, impatiently.

This time, there was no reply.

Jamie looked at his sister.

She was staring intently across the room...

...her eyes open wide with bewildered wonder...

...and then, she slowly raised an arm and pointed...

Chapter 7

The curious, white crystal pyramid under the window was beginning to shrink...or, rather, dissolve into the air like a sugar cube in boiling water. As it vanished, delicate plumes of purple vapour wound upwards...these, too, eventually fading away.

Jessica and Jamie looked at one another and then gingerly approached a black, circular mark on the carpet.

"Cor! It's burnt the floor!" exclaimed Jamie.

It was true! Amid the carpet's pinky flowery design was a singe mark about the size of a dinner plate!

"It's a good job whatever-it-was didn't burn a hole straight through the floorboards!" he went on. "It would have given dad one heck of a shock if he was in his den!"

But it wasn't the burn mark itself that puzzled Jessica.

She was trying to make sense of a strange pattern of sparkling, lighter marks that lay across the charred patch of carpet.

"Look! It's some kind of print!" she pointed, moving her finger around its edge. "Can you see the swirls of lines like a gigantic finger-print...

but in the shape of a huge letter '*S*'...almost as wide as the burn?"
Jamie nodded and looked at his sister.
"Come on, sis!" he insisted. "We've got to get going! All of this
magic *must* have something to do with *Aqua Crysta*! We've got to
get there!"
Jessica was still miles away, staring at the mysterious patch of
blackened carpet.
"It's as though..." she murmured uncertainly under her breath, as if
hidden ears were listening. "It's as though someone has been in here
while we were away...searching all over the room for something...in
every nook and cranny, trying to find...!"
"The crystalid eggs?" wondered Jamie.
Jessica shook her head.
"I don't think so," she whispered. "Something more important!
Something vital!"
She looked through the window dreamily.
"But then again, it could just be my imagination! It's just that I've got
this strange fee...!"
Suddenly, the hairs on the back of their necks stood upright and waves
of tingling, prickling goosebumps swept over their arms and legs
and up and down their spines.
They both listened intently in the silence.
Then they heard it!
Faint, echoey laughter...coming from somewhere above their
heads...from one of the corners of the ceiling!
Haunting, hollow, menacing laughter!
It became louder and louder...and then it faded...faded away to
nothing...only to start again in the opposite corner, then above the
window, then above the dressing-table and the wardrobe.
The manic, chilling laughter seemed to be swelling and fading all over
the room!
Jamie dashed over to the bedside drawers and quickly jerked open the
top drawer, hoping that the brilliant light would pour out again and

reveal their ghostly guest...but the swollen crystalid cocoons just lay there, still and dormant.

There was no light.

No help.

But at least...yes! The laughter had stopped.

Silence returned.

But then, terrifyingly, the children felt cool draughts of air on their faces, the red lamp-shade hanging from the ceiling began to sway...

Something was swirling, sweeping and swooping invisibly around them, fingering their hair and clothes.

They stood, rooted to the spot, frozen with fear, gripped by terror.

They felt like rocks in a whirlpool, trees in a whirlwind - breathless, swamped in swirling air, drowning on dry land!

Just then, thankfully, the air slowly became calm and still.

The children's thudding hearts slowed down.

They breathed more easily.

They looked around with wide eyes.

To their immense relief, the red lamp-shade hanging from the ceiling had stopped moving.

The guest had gone...or was he, she...or it...just hiding?

One thing was for sure!

There was no time to lose!

They had to get going!

"Meet you downstairs in two minutes!" burst Jessica. "Bring your torch and Tregarth's silent-flute! I'll bring the crystalid cocoons in my backpack! We'll be in *Aqua Crysta* in next to no time!"

As the grandfather clock in the hall struck six-o'clock, Jessica and Jamie were almost on their way.

"Now remember, I'm going to have an early night tonight as I'm setting the alarm for quarter to four tomorrow morning!" Mr Dawson reminded them as they pulled their backpacks over their shoulders.

"It won't be dark until way after ten, but I'd like you back here before then, OK? Have you got your maps and plenty to eat and drink?"

Jessica and Jamie nodded and tapped their backpockets to check their folded up maps.

"I'm really looking forward to seeing *'Sunrise at Stonehenge'* on the telly, even if it is at the unearthly time of *four o'clock!*" enthused Mr Dawson, with a smile. "I'll tape it for you...unless, of course, you want to get up and join me for a very early breakfast!"

"We'll see how we feel when we get back, dad!" said Jessica. "Laying one of these treasure-trails takes a bit of effort, you know!"

"They *do!*" admitted their father. "I should know, I've set enough of them for you two! I'll tell you what! As the weather's set fair, why don't you sleep at that old farm of yours tonight. I'm sure you'll be warm enough if you just pack an extra pullover each...and you've probably got enough grub to last you a fortnight, anyway!"

Jessica and Jamie looked at one another, both thinking exactly the same thing.

They knew that they were in for another adventure...and their dad's suggestion could give them more time, if they needed it!

And, if not, it meant a night sleeping out, in the middle of the forest! Fantastic!

"Thanks dad, that'll be great!" burst Jamie. "We might just take you up on that!"

"We'll just get some extra clothing and a drop more water!" said Jessica. "Just in case!"

So, five minutes later, the two children were striding down the green track towards the forest, both of them wearing yellow T-shirts, pale blue denim shorts and their usual battered, fluorescent trainers...each carefully threaded with a couple of small blue jay feathers to bring good luck.

Jessica, for once, had her long copper hair up in a bun, secured with a flowery scrunchie which sprouted even more feathers...longer, fluffy rainbow coloured ones. Jamie's mop of curly ginger hair was more bushy than ever, and he was already beginning to wish that he'd had it cut!

"Phew! I'm boiling and we've only just started!" he gasped. "It's early evening now and it's *still* hot!"

"You'll be OK once we get under the trees!" assured his sister. "It'll be nice and cool in there!"

They both turned and gave their father a final wave before he disappeared indoors. A moment later, they could hear the heavy rhythms  and the wailing guitar of Jimi Hendrix spilling out of *Deer Leap's* open windows. Their father always played his 1960s music at full volume when his children weren't around!

"In two minutes he'll be having a nice cold beer in the back garden!" laughed Jessica, as the green track petered out into a miniature forest of ferns and tall, purply pink foxgloves.

Just beyond was their own secret, narrow path which lead to the tumbled down, half-buried stone wall...the one they'd discovered the August before...the one that had held those first two tiny silver droplets...the tankard and the horn...that had started their wonderful year long adventure!

Their father's music faded away as they delved beneath the towering spruce trees with trunks as wide as dustbin lids. Now they could only hear birdsong...especially the faint tell-tale, hiccupy song of a distant cuckoo.

They scrambled over the gently, sun-dappled drifts of pine-needles until they came to the wall, which they followed to the old, moss covered gate-posts with the rowan tree...now fully in leaf but without the bunches of bright scarlet berries they'd seen on that first occasion. They stopped for a rest and couldn't help gazing into its branches, just

in case they caught sight of
some harvesting Aqua Crystans
with their tiny silver baskets...
although they knew perfectly
well that it was too early for
them to be collecting berries!
Here, the shaded spruce lands
had given way to sun-lit, bright
green larch trees with their
delicate cones, soft needles and tufty pink flowers...all above waves of
lush, long grass. And of course, more sunlight meant more
flowers...yellow celandine, red campion, white stitchwort with splashes
of sky blue forget-me-not, speedwell and darker clumps of bluebells.
The buzzing of busy insects filled the air, together
with the songs of chaffinches and greenfinches. And
somewhere was a woodpecker drumming away at a
tree, maybe its rapid tapping sending coded
messages through the woods.
It certainly was a beautiful Summer's evening!
The children sat under the rowan tree, leaning on a
gate-post each, nibbled home-made flapjacks and
sipped cold orange-juice from plastic bottles rattling
with quickly shrinking ice-cubes.
"We'll be at the quarry soon...and then the old stone barn!" said Jamie,
unzipping a banana.
"And then...*Old Soulsyke Farm!*" beamed Jessica with a wide smile
across her face. "I can't wait to get there,
and see *Verax* again!"
"Let's...just...hope...its still there!"
struggled Jamie, trying to talk and
eat at the same time.
"Oh, it'll be *there* alright!" burst Jessica,
thinking of the gleaming dagger that the

wizard Merlyn had left on top of her brother's birthday cake only a few weeks before. "We hid it well enough! Nobody could possibly find it!"

At the small quarry they had another rest perched on the rim of the rocky hollow which nestled in the midst of the cooler, darker sprucelands. The cauldron of gorse, brambles, nettles and fern spread beneath them with just the odd jagged island of orangy-brown rock breaking the greenery, like dumplings in a great bowl of broth. "It reminds me of *'Stig of the Dump'*!" smiled Jessica, thinking of the book Miss Penny was reading to them at school.

"You never know! Perhaps another hermit lives down there!" said Jamie, taking the opportunity to delve into his backpack for a ginger biscuit. "In that cave at the bottom of the little cliff over there!"

Jessica glanced at the small, dark opening as she pulled on her backpack. "We must come and explore some...!"

Suddenly, Jamie grabbed her arm.

"Sshh! Did you hear that?" he whispered, looking behind into the dark ranks of spruce trees. "I'm sure I heard a twig crack!"

"It'll just be a squirrel...or a deer!" replied Jessica, peering into the shadows. "Come on, let's get going!"

"Listen! I tell you I can hear something!" insisted Jamie.

Then they both heard it!

The distinct sound of crunching undergrowth!

Another crunch...then another!

Footsteps in the forest!

More twigs cracked, one after the other!

Nearer and nearer!

And then...

...a sound that made their blood run cold...

...the haunting cackle of laughter!!

Chapter 8

They knew exactly what it was! The same terrifying, menacing sound they had heard back at *Deer Leap*! But now it was here, with them, in the depths of the forest! It had followed them! The two of them stood like statues, their hearts thudding, beads of sweat glistening on their foreheads.

The haunting sound was there, but, again, there was nothing to see except the never-ending dark columns of tree trunks towering from a brown sea of pine-needles.

They were alone...and scared!

The first time ever in their forest.

The forest that had seemed so welcoming and friendly...until now!

Suddenly, the laughter faded...only to burst out again behind them.

They instantly turned...but again, there was nothing to see!

The laughter was somehow hovering in mid-air above the quarry, its ghostly, mocking sound coming from no-one!

Then...even worse...they felt the warm air beginning to move around them.

It suddenly began to chill.

The long grass by their feet began to sway.

As they gazed into the quarry below, the bushes of gorse and bramble began to rustle, the ferns and nettles began to wave!

It was as if the quarry had been hit by a sudden swirling wind!

The tranquility of the hollow vanished in an instant!

Its greenery began to toss and tumble from side to side, like the sea in a storm ravaged harbour. Bushes beat against the orangy-brown cliffs and lapped angrily against the jagged rocky islands.

The laughter became louder and louder, seeming to fill the entire open mouth of the quarry, echoing from side to side!

Louder and louder...

...until it stopped abruptly, as if the invisible tormentor had run out of breath!

The quarry became calm, the air warmed.

The sun shone on the children's faces...but did nothing to relieve their fears.

There was only one thing they could do!

They grabbed their backpacks and ran!!

On and on, until they reached the shelter of the remaining walls of the ruined old barn.

They fell, gasping and panting, into its last corner...hoping and praying that they had lost their terrifying, invisible pursuer!

Jessica peeped over the rough stones and looked for any signs, not that there would be anything to see! Thankfully, everything seemed normal...buzzing hoverflies, butterflies, birdsong, sunshine...and not a

trace of that fearsome laughter or the wind that gusted from nowhere!

As their hearts slowed, they took comfort in the knowledge that they were directly above *Aqua Crysta*!

The township of Pillo was deep, deep down in the rocks below...
safely away from the horrors of the Upper World.

From where they were in the ruins, Jessica and Jamie could just see the
top of the old waterpump...and they knew that its pipe lead straight
down to the magnificent Pillo Falls. They even managed a smile when
they thought of the time last Summer when they'd helped Jonathan and
Jane pump the magical, frothy water up from the River Floss...and then
used it to shrink the three monstrous earthmovers that were threatening
the Harvestlands and *Aqua Crysta* itself!

"Do you remember the wisp of blue smoke we saw here last August?"
asked Jessica, looking at the pile of fallen rocks just beyond the remains
of the wooden door frame.

"And the smell...the scent of roasted chestnuts!" Jamie added, licking
his lips. "Drifting up from Pillo
through cracks in the rock!"

They then thought of the sad, old,
rusted tricycle that they had buried
under the same pile of rocks...the
tricycle that had once belonged to
Jonathan and Jane when they had
lived at *Old Soulsyke* after being
evacuated from London during the
Second World War.

Thoughts of their friends down in *Aqua Crysta* stirred them to their feet.
"Come on, little brother! Let's make tracks!" said Jessica. "Let's get to
Old Soulsyke! I'll feel safer there!"

With many anxious glances into the dark shadowy
depths of the forest, they made their way to the ruined farm.

They half-expected, at any moment, to hear the cackling laughter or feel
the air chill around them. It seemed so strange to be walking through the
trees feeling worried and nervous. Until now, the forest they had named
George had been a good friend. Now, they felt they couldn't trust it...as
though they had discovered something dark and sinister in its character.

It made them feel uncomfortable...and thoughts about sleeping out overnight had *definitely* disappeared! They could hardly wait to climb down the well and reach the warm, familiar, friendly safety of *Aqua Crysta*!

Soon they were scrambling up the heathery bank that lead to *Old Soulsyke* and its wonderful copse of broadleaf woodland. As they rested at the top and gazed into the sun drenched beauty of oaks, sycamores, horse chestnuts and beeches, they instantly began to feel more at ease and less anxious.

The magic of the place was amazing!

It was so warm and inviting, with a whole chorus of birdsong to welcome them, lead by red-breasted robins and excitable, darting wrens. A glorious canopy of leaves billowed above them, made up of every shade of green you could imagine...all held up by dozens of ancient, sturdy trunks. It was like looking into a vast cathedral...a cathedral of nature, built of trees instead of stone!

The magic drew the children in.

They crunched through the bright golds and yellows of fallen leaves that thickly carpeted the floor, passed the familiar walnut tree and entered the walled, paved farmyard of *Old Soulsyke*.

They were there at last!

They felt safe here!

They breathed sighs of relief.

After dropping their backpacks in the dry stone trough by the doorway, they quickly found the old ladder they had hidden behind the deserted farmhouse. They carried it into the gloomy cool of the building and propped it up to reach the square hole in the ceiling. A moment later they were both up in the loft...their own private den in the depths of the forest!

It was divided into two rooms by a wall of newer stone and wooden boards that didn't quite reach the ceiling. One room had the remains of stained, flowery wallpaper peeling off...the other was just white plaster, with a hole in the roof through which rays of sunlight sliced through the darkness. Neither of the rooms had proper windows just a couple of small square holes at floor level about a foot across. "I think we'd better get a torch!" suggested Jessica, as she looked into the darkest corner of the wallpapered room. "We've got to

find that loose stone in the wall where we hid *Verax*!"

"I'll nip down and get mine!" said Jamie. "Won't be a sec!"

A moment later, Jessica was left all alone in the dark loft of *Old Soulsyke*. Normally, she wouldn't have thought anything of it...but today...well today, things seemed different!

And it wasn't long before the icy cold fingers of fear began to grip her, as she sat there on the floor, in the dark!

She shuffled over to one of the little holes in the wall and took a little comfort from the bright sunlit scene beyond the farmyard.

But it wasn't enough.

Her nerves were getting the better of her.

What if the ghostly laughter started again...and this time she was by herself...in the dark?

What if...?

It was then that she heard it!

On the roof!

A sudden clatter!

On the tiles directly above her head!

Something was moving!

A scratching, scraping sound!

It reminded her of the noises she'd heard in the top drawer, back in her bedroom at *Deer Leap*!

The noise stopped...

...then started again!

She was beginning to feel cold.

She shivered, a rash of goosebumps spread over her arms.

"*JAMIE!*" she called shakily. "*Jamie*!! *Are you there?*"

"What's up, sis? You nearly made me fall down the blinkin' ladder!!"
Her brother's mop of ginger hair suddenly appeared through the hole in
the floor. She'd never been as glad to see it!

"Are you OK?" he asked, looking at his sister curiously. "You know
what? I've just seen a squirrel jump straight onto the roof of this place
from the branch of a tree! It must have jumped a clear five metres!
Are you sure you're alright? It was one heck of a shout! Frightened me
to death!"

"Er..oh, I...I just wanted you to bring my backpack! Th...that's it...my
backpack! So I can check the crystalids are OK!...OK?"

"Great minds think alike!" grinned Jamie, dragging up Jessica's red
backpack behind him. "Fish around for your torch first and then we'll
check on the little critters!"

Soon, torchlight flooded the loft (much to Jessica's
relief) and Jamie crawled over to the corner and felt the long loose stone
in the wall that concealed Merlyn's dagger.

Carefully, he gripped the sides of the stone and began to edge it forward.
With a rough, grating sound it inched outwards, until it was ready to be
lifted from the wall.

"Jess, you'll have to give me a hand!" he called over his shoulder.

"It's too heavy!"
Jessica was just about to open the
box of crystalid cocoons.
"OK, I'm coming!"
She quickly joined her brother and
together they lifted the stone from
the wall and lowered it gently to the
floor.

And there, stood on its side at the back of the dark recess, facing them...in all its glory...was the wonderful gift that the wizard had left in *Deer Leap's* kitchen just a few short weeks before.

Its great, golden handle and sapphire studded hilt glinted in the torchlight, its shaft enclosed in an elaborately patterned brown leather sheath.

It was absolutely magnificent!

Jessica reached into the rectangular hole...and was just about to lift the amazing dagger from its hiding place when...

...they both heard a peculiar swishing noise behind them!

Then another!

And another!

Like whiplashes, or swords cutting through swathes of silk!

The two children turned and gazed back into the loft.

And there before them was a sight they had dreaded seeing...

a small pyramid of white crystal, gently glowing in the dark!

The air began to move.

It began to swirl around, blowing all the plaster dust and leaves in the loft into little spinning whirlwinds.

Then it grew colder, and the children felt the chilling wind fingering their clothes and hair.

But this time there was no laughter!

Just a haunting whisper hovering above the hole in the floor.

"*That is what I seek!*" the invisible phantom breathed, triumphantly.

"*That is what I seek!*" it hissed.

"*Verax is mine!*"

"*Verax is mine!*"

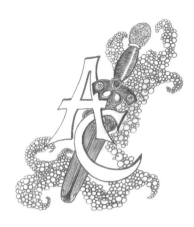

Chapter 9

The whole, gloomy loft seemed to fill with hissing, sizzling whispers, as the words '*Verax is mine!*' were repeated over and over again, echoing from one wall to the other and becoming louder and louder...louder and louder!

At the same time, more and more whiplash swishes scored the air, which began to seethe into such a wild tempest, that its victims were forced to cling to one another, as the icy gale raged around the ancient rafters and beams. So furious did the gale become that even the incessant whispers were drowned by its ghostly, whistling howl.

Then, as the petrified children cowered and tried to shield themselves, the invisible wraith struck!

It took what it wanted!

Its arms gusted their way past Jessica and Jamie and grasped the dagger. *Verax* floated from its hiding place...paused in mid-air, supported by unseen hands...then swooped over the heads of the two children...and hovered over the hole in the floor.

The gale became a wind...and then a breeze.

The howling vanished, the swishing sounds ceased...just the manic whispering remained.

'*Verax is mine!*'

'*Verax is mine!*'

Jessica looked at the pyramid of white crystal...and then she noticed the unopened box of crystalid cocoons by her backpack.

It was moving!

She could hear the same scratching and scraping noises she'd heard in her top drawer!

Once again, something was happening to the crystalids!

One thought instantly crossed her mind!

But the box was just out of her reach.

The invisible phantom would see her!

The thought pounded away in her head.

Dare she do it?

However fearsome the result, she *had* to do it!

Yes!

She suddenly summoned all the courage she had, and with her heart thudding fiercely in her throat and ears, she threw herself across the floor!

With an outstretched arm, her finger-tips nudged the lid off the box!

The loft was flooded with the same bluish-green light as before!

But what it revealed was a hundred...no, a thousand...times more horrifying than the last time!

The two children gazed into the loft, dumbstruck.

The solid, crazy crystal slashes were everywhere, drawn manically all over the rooms, like a child's wild scribbling!

But it was what was hovering menacingly before them, only feet away, that made the blood in their veins almost turn to ice!

The creature was awesome!

Like nothing ever witnessed or conjured up by the most vivid of imaginations!

It was a shapeless, almost transparent, swirling mass of deep purple and maroon vapour or gas, floating in the air, constantly changing form, like a drop of ink in a slightly shaken jar of water.

It was as high as the roof and as wide as the loft. It shimmered as it swirled, as if the gas was filled with fine crystal powder. Its many swaying, slithering limbs, like flames from a churning, purple fire, licked the air hungrily.

Two of the smoky, writhing arms held the dagger, its gold glimmering and glistening against the purple. In the centre, where the vapour was at its densest, a pair of dark orange eyes with red pupils stared outwards, relishing the treasure. Each as large as a dartboard, swelling and shrinking, stretching this way and that, as the formless cloud swirled and whirled.

Beneath the eyes lay a monstrous, toothless, lipless mouth...gaping wide open, twisting and turning into one shape after the other.

The whole thing just hung there, billowing and churning, shimmering and swirling...as though it was uncertain what to do next.

Then, as if suddenly aware of its own visibility, the creature's eyes took on a look of anger, it mouthed one last '*Verax is mine!*' and began to whirl and spin into a purple, funnel-shaped tornado centred above the pyramid of white crystal. It then shrank into the small, glassy mound, almost as if it was being sucked in!

A moment later, nothing of it, nor the precious dagger, remained.

The fearsome phantom had gone!

The pile of crystals on the floor glowed for one last time... and then dissolved into nothing. A few thin wisps of purple vapour drifted upwards and, once again, a circular patch of charred floor appeared with the letter '*S*' etched into the black.

Jessica and Jamie looked at the crystalid box.

The cocoons were perfectly still and calm. No bigger, no smaller...just the same. As their light slowly faded and disappeared, so too, did the maze of aerial crystal lashes that had criss-crossed the loft.

Soon, there wasn't a trace left of any of them.

Everything was back to normal...or so the children thought!

"Come on, Jamie!" urged Jessica, now anxious to leave *Old Soulsyke* behind. "We'll be at the well in less than an hour...then at long last we'll be safe!!"

She carefully slid the crystalid box into her backpack and they both glanced sadly into the corner of the loft where they had hidden *Verax.*

"Will we ever see it again?" Jamie wondered, as he put his foot on the top rung of the ladder, and started to climb down.

"Hang on, what's up?" he burst. "I can't get my leg through the hole!"

"Ow!" groaned Jessica, "I've just knocked my head on something! Something that's not there!"

Jamie banged his foot in the space across the hole in the floor, as though he was trying to break ice on a frozen puddle. He was hitting something...but there was nothing there!

Jessica slowly waved her arms in the air, as though she was feeling her way in pitch blackness.

"There's one...and another!" she exclaimed. "The place is full of those solid crystal swirls...but I can't see any of them!"

"Then it must be solid, invisible crystal across the hole!" said Jamie.

"Are you sure? Let me have a go!"

Jessica stamped on the hole...but nothing happened.

Then they both stood in the middle of the space, as if they were standing on thick plate-glass!

"I can't believe it!" gasped Jamie. "We can't get down!"

"And there's no other way out!" sighed Jessica, looking anxiously at her brother. "We're *trapped*!!"

Meanwhile, deep down in the peaceful, tranquil world of *Aqua Crysta*, there was a stirring...a wakening...a realisation that something was wrong...way above...in the Upper World.

Quentin noticed it first...and then Toby...the two elders sat at their table half-way up the Larder Steps.

They were the *Guardians of Lumina*...the eternal flame that had danced for centuries above her never melting candle.

The slender flame and her fine, weaving plume of smoke had begun to quiver. Then the flame had shrunk, squatted and shot upwards, stabbing the warm air.

Quentin and Toby instantly knew the signs.

The flame's erratic behaviour was a warning.

Lumina was telling them that something in the Upper World was threatening their beloved Kingdom.

"Whatever we do, we do not want to panic and upset everyone during the celebrations and festivities!" murmured silver-bearded Quentin, as he sat on his stool staring at the flickering flame.

"But we must observe *Lumina* with all due diligence, my friend," insisted his companion, the rather rotund Toby, "and if we feel that it is necessary to inform Her Majesty, then that is precisely what we should do! After all, it is almost *Midsummer Night*, up there in the Harvestlands, and...!"

"...we *all* know what *that* means!" Quentin finished, casting his gaze upwards.

"Precisely!" agreed Toby, also glancing up into the Floss Cavern's roof.
                         Quickly they returned to the vital business at hand, and resumed their watch. The candle flame at once plumed gracefully, but then swayed and fluttered as though a gentle breeze was caressing her.

"She *is* certainly distressed!" sighed Quentin, his large blue eyes like pools set in his pale, sallow skin, and both reflecting *Lumina*.

"Look, my friend," said the rosy-cheeked Toby, "you are as aware as I, that the spirits and demons of the Forest are at large on this particular evening in the Upper World. Do you agree?"

Quentin nodded.

"We have witnessed it all before!" reassured Toby. "No harm will befall us...it never does!"

The two elders sat and said nothing for a moment, then Quentin looked intensely into his friend's eyes.

"Unless, of course," he whispered, almost not wanting to mention the name, "Unless, of course, it is...the *Shym-ryn*...that is up and about in the Harvestlands!"

Toby shuddered at the thought, and considered his companion's words. "Then that would be a different matter...," he finally admitted, his usually beaming face turning grim, "...a *very different* matter, indeed!"

But for the time being, they sat and stared at their charge, wondering whether or not to sound the alarm and bring the festivities to an end. It was a tricky decision, and one that taxed them. If one of the nastier forest demons was to get up to mischief...or worse...then there could well be a high price to pay...especially if it *was* the dreaded *Shym-ryn*!

On the other hand, the Harvestlands had been plagued by spirits and demons for centuries, usually on *Midsummer Night*...and although nothing too threatening and serious had ever happened...there had always been talk and stories of one or two incidents that put fear into the hearts of all Aqua Crystans, every time they heard them! But no-one was ever sure if the tales were fact or fiction, truth or myth! Especially those regarding the *Shym-ryn*!

The candle flame suddenly began to dance even more erratically! Quentin and Toby looked at one another, and decided there and then that something *had* to be done!

Together, they reached for their silver horns that hung from golden rope belts around their ample waists...and blew, in unison, three long alarm notes.

The notes echoed up and down the Cavern, sending their message to other hornblowers posted at intervals northwards to Pillo and southwards to Galdo.

Just moments later, every single Aqua Crystan in the realm came to a halt and froze! Even those up in the Forest Cellar, or

the *Palace of Dancing Horses*. They were nearly at the top of the well and closest to the dangers of the Upper World.

Everyone throughout the Land stopped what they were doing and anxiously looked at whoever they were standing next to.

Those left in Pillo (remember, most had gone to Galdo) sat perfectly still at the tables of the town's famous harbour-side eating establishments such as *Dolbetti's, Calzo's* and the *Magpie Inn*.

'DOLBETTI'S' — PILLO

All the customers quietly sipped from their goblets of bramble wine and nibbled the scrumptious foods. They gazed across the waters at the great, curved rocky wall that towered above them. At the moment there were just the odd few thin ribbons of water trickling from the top...but soon the great Pillo Falls would tumble and plunge sending waters down the Floss Cavern to Galdo.

People calmly considered what to do.

Hearing the alarm horns in *Aqua Crysta* was a rare occurrence.

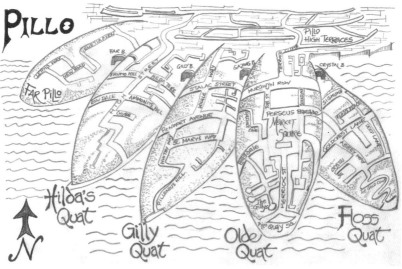

Quentin and Toby were certainly
not known for over-reacting.
So, the conclusion of everyone
in Pillo was the same. Whether
they be down by the harbour, at
home in one of the Quats (the

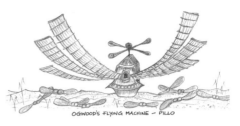

OGWOOD'S FLYING MACHINE – PILLO

four quarters of the town) or maybe at the Museum, or at the Ogwood's
Flying Machine Memorial Park...they would gather by the quayside and
await the *Goldcrest*.

All two hundred or so remaining Pillonians would then be ferried to the
Meeting Hall Cavern. That was the usual procedure, and, by now,
everyone at the festivities in Galdo would be making their way calmly to
the same place, too.

And, indeed, that was exactly what was happening at
the far end of the Floss Cavern. The market stalls, picnic-spots and
spiralling pathways were being deserted in a slow, orderly fashion. Aqua
Crystans were already climbing aboard a variety of small vessels moored
along Galdo's small pier, and dozens of long rowing boats, holding up to
twenty or thirty passengers, were heading across the still waters of *Lake
Serentina*. One by one the boats entered the current of the Floss and were
swept along the river on their short journeys to the *Meeting Hall Cavern*.

In one such craft sat Queen Venetia, Lepho and
Jonathan and Jane.

"When we are all gathered, I shall speak to the people!" said the Queen
quietly to her trusted advisor, Lepho. "Some strange, unknown
happening is occurring in the Upper World!"

"All the magic that we have witnessed suggests that you are correct, your
Majesty!" said the Mayor of Pillo.

As the boat picked up speed, the Queen's long, golden hair flowed
behind in the breeze.

"And I feel certain," she went on, "that our friends, Jessica and Jamie,
are on their way here to join us!"

She looked intently at Lepho, Jonathan and Jane.

"I just hope that they come to no harm!"

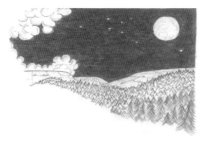 Back at *Old Soulsyke*, the two trapped children were sitting hunched up in the middle of the loft's dusty floor, gazing blankly through the square hole into the downstairs room. All was dark and gloomy, but still warm. The sun had dipped beneath the trees three hours ago, to be replaced by a full moon.

Midnight had come and gone.

The children had drifted in and out of sleep for what seemed like ages and ages...it was now just after one o'clock in the morning!

They had spent over *five* long, long hours in the invisible crystal web woven by the fearsome vapour.

The strange, transparent barrier across the hole was impenetrable.

Jamie had even dropped the large stone from the wall onto it, but the stone had just landed with a clatter, with not so much as a tiny crack appearing!

But at least they had heard no more of the creature's haunting laughter and hissing whispers. It seemed as though it was satisfied with having found the golden dagger, *Verax*...and had retired to its den or lair to admire the stolen treasure.

"I am convinced that it was looking for Merlyn's dagger in my bedroom before we returned this afternoon," mumbled Jessica, sipping from her water-bottle, "and then it followed us here!"

"Well, whatever it did, I hope we don't come across it again!" grumbled Jamie, banging his foot for the umpteenth time on the strange, invisible barrier that the creature had somehow laid across the hole. "If only we could smash our way through!"

Jessica crawled over to one of the small gaps in the wall and peered down into the farmyard. When they had arrived it had been bathed in bright sunshine, but now it was silvery and shadowy, just lit by moonlight.

The magical sight instantly made her think of a poem she'd learned at school...

"*Slowly, silently, now the moon*," she sighed dreamily, dangling her arm out into the cooling air, "*Walks the night in her silver shoon*...I wish I could squeeze through here...!"

"No chance of that, sis!" burst Jamie with a grin. "It'd have to be twice as big before you could get through! And anyway, it's one heck of a drop to the farmyard! You'd do your ankle in if you were lucky! If you were *unlucky*, you'd break a leg...or worse! That's the trouble with the hole in the roof! Even if we could reach it, what do we do, stuck up there?"

"Perhaps the transparent crystal stuff over the hole will dissolve soon," suggested Jessica, as she crawled back to her brother.

"Oh yeah! And pigs might fly! Grunt, grunt!" laughed Jamie.

"Talking of which," smiled Jessica, "I suppose you're getting a bit peckish, aren't you?"

"Peckish? I could eat a horse!" gasped Jamie. "But most of the grub's in *my* backpack! And where's that? In the trough down th...!"

"Sshh! What's that!" whispered Jessica suddenly.

"What's what?"

"Listen! There it goes again!"

A soft purring sound was coming from below.

Then they saw a long shadow glide across the room.

"It must be! *It is*! *It's Spook*!" whispered Jessica.

Slowly and serenely, the sleek white cat came into view and sat gracefully in the middle of the downstairs floor.

The two children eagerly watched, wondering what was going to happen next!

Would its tail twitch?

Would they be swept into its amazing magic once again?

Spook lifted a paw and licked it.

Then the emerald eyes looked upwards and met theirs.

Spook lifted the other paw and licked that.

Then...it happened!

The long, slender, snowy tail twitched once, twice...

.........and a third time!

Chapter 10

What happened next was absolutely incredible!
Unbelievable!
The children were totally dumbstruck with astonishment!
Spellbound and utterly astounded!
From where they were, crouched by the square hole in the floor of the loft, Jessica and Jamie looked down upon a scene of pure magic and amazement!
The silvery darkness of the night had vanished!
Bright daylight had returned in an instant!
Sunlight was flooding through the windows.
But, not only that, the whole of the downstairs room had been transformed in a moment!
Gone was the bare, stony, rubble strewn floor of a deserted, abandoned farmhouse. Instead was a living, breathing room, full of all the signs that it was someone's home!
Almost directly below, just by the foot of the now freshly painted, dark green ladder, was a huge rectangular, wooden

table. In the middle was a small, delicate cut-glass vase packed with bluebells. There was an oval breadboard with half a brown loaf and a carving knife. By it were jars of jam and honey, a flowery butter-dish, white salt and pepper pots, a vinegar bottle...all surrounded by three meal settings with knives, forks and spoons and colourful, circular place-mats of the same design as the butter-dish.

Next to one place-setting was a half open box of matches and a chubby old pipe on its side, with black tobacco ash spilling out onto the well-scrubbed table. By another was a small, bright green tin toy... a clockwork, old-fashioned racing car with its dashing, goggled driver and his green scarf stiffly flying behind. The toy's shiny, silver key was lying by its side, next to the fork, all ready to wind life into the model's coiled spring. And by the third setting was a pink jumble of unfinished knitting, clinging to two long, grey knitting-needles with a ball of pink wool about the size of a small melon sitting on the very edge of the table.

Two wooden chairs were pushed under the table, but the third, with its floral cushion, was out. It was the one by the knitting. Spook the cat was now sitting gracefully on it, still busily licking one of its paws as though nothing had happened!

All at once, its large green eyes noticed the ball of wool.

Playfully, Spook pawed the soft ball and it tumbled silently to the floor and rolled under the table, held to the knitting by a single, thick thread of pink. A second later the cat pounced off the chair and onto the wool, disappearing from view.

Jessica and Jamie, open-mouthed, gazed around the rest of the room.

The doorway now had a door! A heavy, brown panelled one, with a small square window, a round brass handle and a large, matching key protruding from its keyhole. Beneath it was a tan coloured, well worn doormat and to one side an assortment of muddy working boots, shiny best brown shoes, black wellingtons, sandals and pumps, some adult-sized, some child-sized. Above them, the white plaster wall held half a dozen hooks each draped with different sized outdoor clothing...a man's grey jacket and a brown corduroy hat, children's dark blue raincoats, green overalls, patched up pullovers and scarves.

On the other side of the door, the old, dusty white pot sink now gleamed brightly with a tidy pile of pans drying. Beyond that was a large chunky oven with four coiled electric hobs, one occupied by a fat silver kettle. Above it was a kind of metal rack which held a row of plain white plates of different sizes, all slotted in sideways at an angle, standing on their rims.

Then came a tall, wooden dresser with lines of even more dinner plates, side plates and saucers on show, all facing outwards...this time with fancy flowery designs on them. Beneath them was a host of matching teacups dangling from small hooks above two rather grand teapots, sugar bowls, cake-stands and other pieces of crockery.

In front of the dresser were a pair of comfortable looking easy chairs and a settee, all of the same russet colour and with plenty of tapestry cushions. The suite was gathered around a large, blue rectangular rough peg rug - the only covering on the whole of the orange grey stone-slab floor.

Beyond the rug was a fireplace with a neat pile of logs to the right and a brass set of poker, coal tongs and small shovel to the left.

Across the top was a thick stone mantelpiece which held twisted brass candlesticks at each end and a rather grand silver clock in the middle.

By the fireplace was a small, highly polished wooden table with an old fashioned record-player on top with a great red and gold horn pointing into the room and a winding handle on the side. On the turntable was black, plastic looking disc about the size of a dinner plate and propped up against the carved legs of the table were several more.

The children's eyes moved back over the room. They were quite captivated by their totally unexpected aerial view of this living museum...and it was just beginning to dawn on them who lived there!

There was no doubt about it!

It *had* to be Jonathan and Jane!

And their nasty uncle, of course.

Sometime in the *Nineteen-Fifties*!

Sometime before he'd abandoned *Old Soulsyke*...and his nephew and niece...when the forest had been planted.

Spook had done it again!

It was incredible!

Suddenly, Jessica gave her brother a nudge, her eyes this time exploring the loft all around them.

She slowly stood up, and so did Jamie.

Gone were the crumbling walls and plaster, bare dusty floorboards and holes in the roof!

It was all wallpapered...both rooms...more or less in the same pattern as Jessica had in her bedroom back at *Deer Leap*! Delicate hedgerow flowers, ferns and butterflies.

The beams were painted white.

It all seemed so fresh!

In one bedroom was a lumpy looking single bed with a huge pillow, all covered with a yellow bedspread. Above was a single light bulb with no shade, dangling on a long electric flex from a beam. The floor boards were polished and clean, as were the small chests of drawers and a very narrow wardrobe with a mirror. On a table by the bed was a large white dish and a tall jug...presumably for washing. More men's clothes were draped over a couple of slim chairs and pictures of old time movie stars were drawing-pinned to the walls.

The other room was definitely Jonathan and Janes'! Two single beds stood side by side, both covered in the same yellow bedspreads. There were also the same small chests of drawers as the other room. But it was the things scattered about the room that gave its occupants away!

Crayons, chalks, a blackboard on an easel, drawings on squares of paper, a toy fort with plastic cowboys and Indians guarding the battlements, a toy loom threaded with multi-coloured scraps of wool, a boy's cricket bat and ball, a pair of roller skates.

Between the beds on a bright red rug lay an enormous spinning top, together with a handful of *Beano* and *Dandy* comics...and on one of the

beds was an unfinished game of *Ludo* with a pair of dice spilling out of a small brown shaking cup. But the best thing of all in Jessica's eyes was what was on a shelf just above the other bed. A neat line of almost brand new, hard-back *Famous Five* books by Enid Blyton! "Dad's favourite!" she whispered dreamily, as she stepped into the children's bedroom from the past. "It's all absolutely fantastic! You know, little brother! I'd loved to have lived then, rather than now! You can have all your electric gadgets, your computers, CDs and DVDs! Give me this anytime!"

Suddenly, Jamie called from behind her.

"Wow! Just have a look at this!"

He was crouched by one of the gaps in the wall, gazing over the farmyard.

"It's all *completely* different!" he gasped. "The farm buildings have all got their roofs on, there's a track leading through the trees, there are

sheep and lambs everywhere and...I *don't believe it*! The forest has *disappeared*!!"

"It's because it hasn't been planted yet, silly!" said Jessica, darting over to the tiny, glassless window. "Let's have a look!"

The view over the farm buildings and the ancient broadleaf trees was amazing! There wasn't a single conifer to be seen! Not one single spruce or larch! Just miles and miles of brown heather moorland and fields of short-cropped grass, dotted with more sheep and surrounded by crooked lines of stone walls.

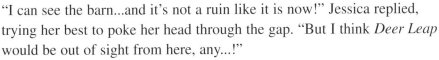

"Can you see the barn with the waterpump?" Jamie asked. "And *Deer Leap*?"

"I can see the barn...and it's not a ruin like it is now!" Jessica replied, trying her best to poke her head through the gap. "But I think *Deer Leap* would be out of sight from here, any...!"

She suddenly stopped.

"Jamie!" she said, with a note of alarm in her voice. "There's a *car* coming along the track towards the farm!!"

"A *what*??"

"A *car*! I tell you there's a *car*...and it's heading straight into the farmyard!"

Jamie nudged his sister out of the way and stared down in total disbelief!

"Let me see again! Am I dreaming? It *is* a *car*, isn't it?" whispered Jessica, pushing her face back into the gap so she was just about cheek to cheek with her brother.

"It *is*! A little, shiny black *Morris Minor* from the 1950s!" gasped Jamie in puzzled admiration. "Registration number...*GBV...803*!"

Both children were mesmerised by the sudden movement in the farmyard...the farmyard that itself had completely changed from how they had known it since they'd discovered *Old Soulsyke* the previous Summer. Gone had all the overgrown, mottled green, mossy paving stones and drifts of fallen leaves. Now, everything was neat and tidy, the paving slabs all clean and pale orange. Hens were wandering about pecking at grain and there were even three goats and a couple of sheep in a wire-mesh pen. Parked next to it was a cart with enormous, wooden spoked-wheels, piled high with bales of hay. And just next to that was something that brought beaming smiles to the children's faces. It was the blue tricycle! All shiny and new, with its blue bell! What a difference from the last time they'd seen it...a rusty, twisted mass of metal buried under the stones of the collapsed barn!

They gazed around the farmyard, both of them completely enchanted and mystified! It was all so strange! The desolate, ruined farmhouse and the broadleaf copse, to Jessica and Jamie, had always been cut-off, inaccessible, surrounded by miles of pine trees! A place hidden and secret.

But now, it was all open and fresh! Alive and looked after! People lived here and it was connected by a track to the moorland lanes and to all that lay beyond.

It was an amazing transformation!

The two children watched as the little car rumbled into the farmyard, the sun glinting off its polished roof. It came to a stop

by one of the small barns. The driver's door opened and out stepped a short, rather round, grey haired man wearing a smart checked jacket, brown cavalry-twill trousers and heavy black boots. He had a harsh looking face, but sounded cheerful.

"C'm'on, you two!" he called in a gruff, Yorkshire accent. "Let's be havin' you! Get y'selves changed and down t' pump! Yon trough's almost empty!"

Then...before the ever-widening, astonished eyes peering down from the farmhouse loft...the back of the driver's seat was pushed forward and two children scrambled out of the car, one after the other.

There was no mistaking them!

Jonathan and Jane!

Looking about eight or nine years old...and both dressed in their 'Sunday Best'outfits! Jonathan, dark haired with rosy cheeks, wearing a checked jacket, checked shirt, thin blue tie, brown corduroy short trousers down to his knobbly knees and long grey socks pulled up so high as to almost meet his trousers! On his feet were a pair of smart looking, light brown sandals. He looked like a miniature version of the man...who, of course, must be the uncle the children had been sent to live with after their parents had died in the bombing of London during the Second World War.

"Just *look* at Jane's frock!" whispered Jessica. "It's beautiful!"

The young girl down in the farmyard was wearing a light blue, finely checked, short-sleeved cotton dress trimmed with swirls of delicate lace. It billowed widely, well below her knees. Jane's face, too, looked rosy and healthy, her dark brown hair loosely flowing down her back, instead of in the ribboned pigtails she always wore in *Aqua Crysta*. On her feet were a pair of sandals similar to her brother's, but accompanied by short, white ankle socks.

Without a word, they both darted across the farmyard, scattering the hens and opened the unlocked farmhouse door. Jessica and Jamie quickly left their tiny window and knelt by the square hole in the loft floor, gazing down into the living room, hoping to see their friends again.

"They look a bit younger than the time we saw them at Sandsend Station!" whispered Jamie.

"That was on the first of July, Nineteen Fifty-Four!" whispered back Jessica. "I reckon this must be a year or two bef...*watch out! They're coming up the ladder!*"

"They'll hit their heads on the crystal stuff over the hole!" gasped Jamie. "They don't know it's there!"

"Stop! Stop!" chorused Jessica and Jamie, as the green ladder began to shake...

...but they needn't have worried...

...the crystal had vanished, dissolved into nothing...

as Jonathan and Jane excitedly clambered into the loft and into their bedroom...straight past their astonished friends from the next century!

"They can't see us or hear us!" whispered Jessica dreamily, watching Jane's every move in her beautiful dress. "It's incredible!"

Then...magically...familiar voices filled the loft!

"I'm sure I left m' ball of wool on the table downstairs, when we left for Whitby!" said Jane, sitting on the edge of her bed unfastening her sandals. "But I've just seen it in the middle of the rug in front of the fire-place! How did it get there? It's as though a cat's had it or something!"

"Never mind that, sis!" laughed Jonathan, undoing his tie. "Just rejoice that Uncle Herbert's in a good mood for a change! He may even let us play with the clockwork toys in the barn!"

"Well, just keep your fingers crossed!" warned Jane. "You know how he changes! Let's get that water double quick and keep him sweet!"

"I think it's all because those guys in the newspapers have just conquered Mount Everest and he's spent a couple of hours watching the Queen's Coronation on that weird, moving picture thing in that Whitby pub!"

"On that *television* gadget, you mean?" laughed Jane. "Mind you, I reckon it was pretty good...watching things going on hundreds of miles away at the very same time as they're happening!"

"With any luck, old misery guts might get one someday, now that he's had electricity put in at last!" said Jonathan. "But, on the other hand, pig's might fly!"

With that, Jessica grabbed her backpack...almost hoping she would be seen...and the silent couple of children from the future slowly began to descend the green ladder. They both had the same mixed feelings! They could have stayed for ever watching and listening to their friends, but they knew that it was all some kind of unexplainable enchantment conjured up by *Spook the cat*...and, at any second now, the whole illusion would vanish into thin air!

And they were right!

By the time they'd both put their feet on the floor of the living room...everything was back to normal!

They were plunged back into the moonlit silver of the night and gone had all the furniture, the wool, the oven, the coats, the wellies...everything! The room had returned to its former, desolate, abandoned self! Even the ladder looked ancient, without a single trace of green paint.

They stepped over the non-existent doormat and tentatively looked into the farmyard. They half hoped they would see the hens, the goats, the sheep, the hay cart, the blue tricycle and, of course, the black, shiny *Morris Minor*...although perhaps *not* Uncle Herbert!

But, *everything* had gone, including the elusive cat, *Spook*...the apparent weaver of all this magic!

Yes, they were disappointed and sad, but at the same time it began to occur to them that they were suddenly free! They had escaped from the crystal web! They could carry on!

Jamie picked up his backpack and nipped behind the farmhouse to grab the all important rope for when they reached the bottom of the well! Soon they would be in *Aqua Crysta*...and, even better, they would be meeting Jonathan and Jane again! But this time, for *real*!!

Chapter 11

By torchlight and moonlight, Jessica and Jamie delved into *George's* deepest, darkest depths. It had been a full six months since they had last ventured beyond *Old Soulsyke*...on that cold, snowy Christmas Eve, and then they'd ridden on the back of the young stag, *Strike*! Jamie thought of trying to summon the deer again by blowing Tregarth's silent flute, but he resisted.

Instead they jogged and walked and scrabbled across the forest...and in less than an hour they'd reached the well. As Jessica sat and rested on a drift of pine-needles, memories of the terrifying red and white flagpole

and the images she'd seen of *Lumina* within the bounds of the Pegasus constellation flooded into her mind. She even looked for the great square of stars in the black sky, but this time she could only make

her way from the Plough, to the North Star and the beginnings of the '*W*' of Cassiopeia. Pegasus wouldn't be visible above the trees for another few weeks.

"At least there's been no sign of fairies, witches and wizards!" laughed Jamie, remembering what Miss Penny had told them at school about *Midsummer Eve*.

"Don't go counting your chickens!" warned his sister, squinting into the darkness between the trees. "And, anyway, I think we've just about had enough of that sort of thing to last us a lifetime, bearing in mind the 'whatever-it-was' that followed us to *Old Soulsyke...*!"

"Not to mention *Spook's* little games!" added Jamie, looking at his watch.

"It's just gone two!" he exclaimed suddenly, almost making his sister jump out of her skin. "In fact, it's a *quarter past two!*"

"Just a bit later than when we jumped into *Aqua Crysta* for the first time, last Summer!" beamed Jessica. "Let's get down there, little brother! Time's getting on! Even dad'll be up in less than a couple of hours to watch his sunrise at Stonehenge on telly!"

Soon, the friendly moon and the silver forest had been left behind as Jessica and Jamie began their descent into *Aqua Crysta*...the cool fragrance of pine replaced by the welcoming, warm, swirling, sweet scent of roasted chestnuts and hazelnuts.

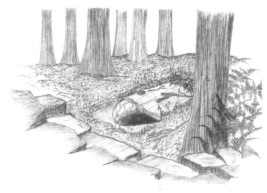

The smell was almost intoxicating, as they carefully stepped from one ancient iron rung to the next.

Then, just as Jamie drew level with the forest cellar...or *The Palace of Dancing Horses*...they both heard the familiar long, eerie tone of a single musical note from a horn. It was coming from deep below their feet.

"They know we're on our way!" whispered Jessica, her heartbeat suddenly speeding up, as excitement and expectation began to bubble wildly in her thoughts. It wouldn't be long before she was once again in the secret, magical, subterranean, crystal world...maybe riding on the *Goldcrest*, seeing Pillo or Galdo, meeting the Queen again, Lepho, and Jonathan and Jane. She could hardly wait!

"I reckon we ought to leave our bags in the forest cellar!" suggested Jamie, clinging onto a rung just opposite the ledge and the door. "We don't even need our torches! The first light from *Aqua Crysta* will be with us soon!"

"But what about the crystalids?" wondered Jessica.

"They'll be safe enough in the cellar until we come back!" replied Jamie, reaching over to the ledge with one of his feet.

"OK then, I guess it'll make things easier!" Jessica agreed. "But remember to take Tregarth's flute. I've just got a feeling we might n...!"

Suddenly, there was such a short, loud crack from Jessica's backpack that both of them nearly lost their grips on the rungs!

It was like gunfire!

Then came another and another!

Then a whole volley of them, like box of firework bangers all going off at once!

"Something's happening to the crystalids!" yelled Jessica, a sudden, icy bolt of fear rushing through her body. As quickly as she could, while hanging on to a rung in Jamie's torchlight, she struggled out of the shoulder straps of her backpack and tossed it onto the ledge.

A moment later, amid even more cracks and bangs, they were both crouching on the ledge pushing on the cellar door. Suddenly, it jolted open with a creaking groan and the two children fell into the rocky, underground room, hoping there were no tiny Aqua Crystans about!

Fortunately, the place seemed deserted as the pair of torchbeams shone on the red, exploding backpack, making it glow fiery red in the darkness of the cellar, its constant crackling and banging ringing in the children's ears.

Then, all at once, the explosions stopped like some kind of cease-fire! Silence filled the room.

Silence almost complete except for a new, quieter, more menacing sound coming from the backpack...a scraping, crunching sound mixed with a peculiar, faint chorus of eerie whines.

Jamie, open-mouthed, pointed at the bag, his torchbeam beginning to shake.

The backpack was moving!

Writhing and squirming as though it had a life of its own!

And, then...it toppled over!

Both children shifted backwards in the cramped space, not for a second taking their eyes off the backpack!

The top flap of the bag suddenly moved!

Something was crawling out of the bag's loosely open neck!

Then, amid a bright fluorescent glow, a pale green, slowly moving liquid began to creep across the gritty floor from beneath the flap, like thick, treacly lava from a volcano.

Jessica and Jamie could hardly believe what they were watching, but what happened next nearly made them pelt through the open door and down the well in double quick time!

A creature began to emerge from under the flap, the like of which had never been seen in the Upper World.

First...a long, pointed, black snout appeared, about the size of a little finger, quivering and twisting as though it was sensing the air.

Then came a head...the size, shape and smoothness of a hen's egg, but shiny black with a pair of bulbous eyes sheathed by closed scaly eye-lids.

The head and snout suddenly reared upwards and shot forwards...and then...in a flash, that sent Jessica and Jamie into one another's arms...the rest of the body appeared...long, black and beetle-like with tightly folded, glassy wings down the sides and dozens of pairs of struggling legs underneath fighting to free the creature from the green, oozy liquid. With one further strain, the hideously ugly beast launched itself from the slime and amid a host of sticky, stretching strings of the green syrup, it scuttled off into the gloom, the pattering sound of its countless scaly legs galloping over the rocky floor echoing between the walls of the cellar.

Jessica and Jamie didn't know where to shine their torches for the best! Onto the mass of clockwork toys and the dolls' house or onto the moving backpack? The thought of another *four* of these monstrous centipedes hatching from the writhing bag made them shudder...and then vanishing into the dark nooks and crannies...or, even worse, scurrying up their own bodies...!

All those creepy-crawly legs! All that disgusting, green, stringy slime! Insects the size of large, fat sausages!

There was suddenly no doubt about it!

They had to get through the door as quickly as possible, shut it firmly...and get down the well!

As the second and third creatures began to struggle through the slime and with torchbeams darting crazily everywhere, the children crawled through the small doorway and onto the ledge.

They turned and glanced back into the cellar.

The torchbeams fell upon two of the giant centipedes scuttling between

the carousel and the helter-skelter into the dark, the scratchy pitter-patter sound of hundreds of legs sending shivers up and down Jessica and Jamie. Then they heard the sound of toys being knocked over as the creatures wove blindly through the fairground.

"Just think of the damage they could do if they get into the dolls' house!" whispered Jessica with a tremor in her voice.

"And just think what could happen if they get into the Harvest Passageway that leads down into *Aqua Crysta*!" gasped Jamie.

With the cellar door safely closed and the torches left on the ledge, the children began the rest of the descent. The first part was a bit

tricky in the dark but, with the rope dangling in two halves, they made quick progress. Soon the first milky light from the magical kingdom began to lap their feet, and it wasn't long before they could make out the welcoming pinky, white disc that was the bottom of the well.

Jamie reached the last rung and gazed into the magical landscape just a couple of metres below. There was the winding, pearly stream only inches across, which he knew to be the great, wide River Floss flowing majestically through the Cavern linking Pillo and Galdo. In a few moments he would be standing on its pebbly shore! Time would stand still, and he would

be there, standing in the middle of the secret, enchanting world!
He looked up at his sister who was busy gathering in the rope.
"Pass it down and I'll thread it over the last rung!" he called, anxious to jump.
He checked his watch.
"It's about five minutes to three!" he called. "The sun'll be up in an hour at Stonehenge, and dad'll be gawping at the telly with a bowl of *Frosties* on his knee!"
"Just hope he remembers to record it!" laughed Jessica. "You know how forgetful he is!"

A couple of minutes later, with the rope dangling through wisps of mist down into the magical valley, Jamie shoved Tregarth's silent flute down the inside of his yellow T-shirt and began the countdown to his jump.

"I want to jump at exactly *three minutes to three!*" he called, teetering on the last rung, ready to push himself off backwards.

"Good luck, little brother!" shouted Jessica. "See you it *Aqua Crysta!* I'll try not to land on you!"

"You'd better not! *Eight...seven!...*Here goes! See you soon! *Five...four...three...two...one...byeeeee!*"

Jamie sprung into the magic...and was gone!

Jessica climbed down to the last rung, touched the jay feathers in one of her trainers for good luck and looked down into the mists at the gradually fading rope. She knew that in a few moments her whole body would have shrunk to the size of her thumb!

She took a deep breath, closed her eyes...

...and she, too, plunged into the magic of *Aqua Crysta*.

There at last! But if they thought that the journey so far had been full of magic and fear...it was *nothing* compared to what was to come! Indeed, it is safe to say that things would *never, ever...be the same again!! Never...ever!!*

Chapter 12

By now, virtually the whole population of *Aqua Crysta* had gathered in the *Meeting Hall Cavern*...just over two thousand Aqua Crystans. Some had come by foot from the nearby villages of Middle Floss and the Heights of Serentina, while others had sailed in small craft from Galdo. Most, however, had arrived on board the splendid *Goldcrest*...and that, of course, included the new arrivals from the Upper World!

It was just a short journey from the shores beneath the well to the *Meeting Hall Cavern*, but it became very clear from the other passengers that Jessica and Jamie were very welcome. Not

'MIDDLE FLOSS'

93

only as Guests of Honour at the cut short celebrations, but also, once again, as some kind of help and support against unknown perils from above!

"Everyone is expecting you!" beamed the dark haired Captain Frumo at the ship's wheel. "Since the alarm horns sounded, every Crystan has made his or her way to the *Meeting Hall Cavern*! Pillo and the Island of Galdo are just about deserted! Mind you, Pillo was deserted anyhow!"

"Why?" asked Jessica, gazing at the glistening white walls of the Floss Cavern rushing by.

"The celebrations and festivities in Galdo!" enthused the Captain. "The *Goldcrest* has never been so busy! Non-stop, this way and that, full load of passengers every journey! But then, of course, came the alarm horns and that put an end to all that! Mind you, I think the Queen and Mayor Lepho will keep spirits up in the *Meeting Hall*!"

Suddenly, Captain Frumo, burst into laughter.

"Not that I should mention '*spirits*', if you know what I mean?" he laughed. "It's always the same at this time in the Upper World year... Midsummer Night and all that! Fairies and demons, witches and wizards! We always have these false alarms and they never come to anything!"

Jessica and Jamie looked at one another and thought they'd better say nothing about the happenings back in the forest. They'd save that particular story for the Queen and Lepho. Best not to panic anyone now, and the same for the strange creatures scuttling about in the *Palace of Dancing Horses*!

Soon, the golden galley with its furled yellow sail was moored by the little rocky pier that jutted out into the Floss. Beyond it was the vast, gaping semi-circular archway that was the entrance to the

Meeting Hall Cavern. Rows of
pointed, pink stalactites hung like
fangs from the top of the arch,
matched by tall, rounded stalagmites
towering from beneath...making the
great hole seem even more like a
monstrous mouth. It seemed to

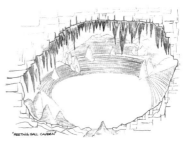

dwarf everything, but it was the bright crystal light from beyond and the
strange silence that drew Jessica and Jamie forward.
"I thought everyone in *Aqua Crysta* was supposed to be here!"
whispered Jamie. "It seems so quiet!"
Captain Frumo, his crew and the rest of the passengers followed behind,
as the the procession made its way along a path and then up a short
flight of steps.
Slowly, the magnificent ceiling of the cavern began to come into view.
It was absolutely packed with stalactites and patches of shining crystals
of all shades of pink and red.
After another short flight of steps, Jessica and Jamie reached a sort
of flat rock shelf...and suddenly, the whole majestic, wonderful
interior could be seen...like a vast Roman amphitheatre, with
great, sweeping arcs of carved terraced seating...all crammed
full with waiting Aqua Crystans dressed in every colour you could
imagine!
And...believe it or not...in front of the banked terraces...in the oval
arena...a *cricket match* was going on! Jamie had to blink twice to make
sure he wasn't dreaming! A cricket match being played in a crystal
cavern deep underground! Stumps, fielders, two batsmen, a bowler, a
wicket-keeper, a scoreboard, umpires...the lot...but not a hint of green
grass to be seen!
A moment later, an enormous din burst out of the silence as though
someone had thrown a switch! It filled the cavern to the brim...not to
mention the ears of the honoured guests! Cheers, singing and hundreds
of calls of welcome echoed throughout the gaping mouth. And not only

that! All at once, the rows upon rows of still figures were suddenly transformed into an animated, waving, dancing crowd!

The normally reserved Aqua Crystans had all gone wild with excitement! Had someone hit a six??

Jessica and Jamie shyly waved from the rocky shelf...and then beamed the widest smiles that had ever illuminated their faces!

They'd noticed on the far side of the huge, glistening arena a small wooden platform...and on it the four unmistakable, waving figures of Queen Venetia, Lepho, Jonathan and Jane!

Without a moment's delay, the two visitors from the Upper World ran down a slope, and across the crystal dust arena and its cricket pitch!

As they neared the podium, the cheers and singing faded away to be replaced by a solid wall of wild applause, so loud that it sounded like the combined waterfalls of Galdo and Pillo!

Then that, too, faded away as the two children climbed the small, wooden steps and hugged their hosts one after the other.

Under the heavy silence that followed...a silence so complete that you could have heard a drip drop...the Queen spoke to her people and her welcome guests. Hundreds of eyes watched her every move as she glided to the front of the platform and faced the great, colourful arc of all her gathered countrymen, women and children.

Her flowing indigo gown, streaked with turquoise, shimmered in the crystal light, as did her cascade of pale, golden hair flowing down her back and her simple coronet of silver, studded with three delicately cut, deep red crystals.

"Our Kingdom has existed in secret for many centuries of Upper World time," she began, "and although our celebrations and festivities on the Island of Galdo have been interrupted, we can still celebrate the arrival of our great friends, Jessica and Jamie!"

Spontaneous applause and cheering rattled round the Hall, and the two children waved in return.

The Queen gracefully raised an arm and her people fell silent.

Again she spoke with a clear, confident voice silhouetted against the solid silence, like a pure white feather on a cushion of black velvet. "It has to be said, however, that, by some magical means, I was expecting them!" she resumed, with a smiling glance at the two visitors. "And, although I wish you all no alarm, I can promise that there is some reason for their visit. Magic is at work! I know not of its nature, but somehow we will be its match!"

Another torrent of applause and cheers sprang from the listening crowd and gushed around the cavern, hushed again by her raised arm.

"And one thing is clear!" she carried on, beaming at her audience. "While we speak and plan, the celebrations *must continue!*"

More applause and cheers!

"Tom Grinkle from Middle Floss is in charge of entertainment! I put you all in his capable hands!"

With that, amid much chatter from the terraces, the platform party walked down the wooden steps and across the arena towards a rocky alcove by one of the enormous stalagmites.

Jamie couldn't resist talking to a couple of the fielders who had sat in the crystal dust listening to Queen, both of them dressed in pale, heather coloured tunics and trousers. One of them, by the name of Dillip Underhill, even tossed Jamie a catch with the ball...a strange hard plaited mixture of grass and bark.

"Can you spin with it?" asked Jamie, eagerly inspecting the ball closely and pretending to bowl. "It's certainly rough enough!"

The other player, Benjamin Carver, laughed.

"We have not yet mastered bowling *straight* at the wickets!" he said.

"You will have to teach us all you know sometime!"

It was then that Jamie noticed the wickets!

"You've got *four* stumps and *three* bails for each wicket!" he exclaimed. "That makes life a lot easier for the bowlers! They've more to aim at!

In the Upper World we only have *three* stumps and *two* bails to bowl at!"
He looked at the scoreboard.
"I see it's Pillo versus Galdo, and Galdo have already made one hundred and sixty-seven for...*how many wickets?*"
"Seventeen!" laughed Dillip.
"We play with teams of twenty men, women, boys and girls in each side, but our captain declared on that score to give Pillo a turn at batting! They have already made ninety-nine for the loss of only *one* wicket! They are doing very well!"
"Galdo could do with your help!" smiled Ben. "Perhaps you could show us your...what do you call it...?"
"Spin bowling!" enthused Jamie, tossing himself a catch. "OK, as long as the Pillo captain doesn't mind!"
"*Jamie*!!" suddenly came Jessica's impatient voice from the alcove. "Come on, we've got important news for the Queen!"
"Let him play!" said the Queen gently. "It is good to see him joining in with my countryfolk. It binds our friendship!"
Jamie walked up to the bowling end of the pitch and looked at the confident Pillo batsman who was standing defiantly with his bat in front of his wicket, ready to face the wizard bowler from the Upper World!
The fielders all got into their positions and crouched, hands ready for a possible catch.
"Let play continue!" one of the umpires announced.
The crowd gazed in expectant silence at the pitch.
What would happen?
Would Jamie be hit for six?
Would he bowl the batsman out?

Jamie glanced again at the batsman, trotted up to the bowling line in four short paces, and bowled...

The ball spun in the air down the pitch like a top, landed in the crystal dust in front of the batsman, spun sharply to the left...missed the batsman's bat and clattered into his stumps, toppling all three bails to the ground!

The batsman looked with a puzzled frown at the pitch, then at his bat and then at his shattered stumps. He had been well and truly bowled by an amazing spinning ball!

The Galdo supporters cheered wildly as the batsman turned, grinned and walked off...to be replaced by the next man...who was, in fact, a woman! She marched boldly towards the pitch dressed in the darker heather strip of the Pillo team. As she marched she swung her bat determinedly, her reputation as a big hitter known to all!

She stood by the restored stumps, tapping the ground with her bat, ready to face the demon spinner from the World above!

Jamie took the ball, tossed himself a catch, ran in...two, three, four paces...and bowled.

Again the ball spun dizzily in the air down the length of the pitch and hit the ground.

The batswoman, named Bella, swung her bat for all she was worth, intent on sending the ball straight into the River Floss for six!

Instead she missed it...the ball spun sharply to the left and hit the stumps. Bella looked in amazement at her stumps lying flat on the ground!

Out for a duck, first ball!

Another wild cheer went up, and the Galdo team mobbed its star bowler, congratulating him on his wizardry!

And so he should have been!

He had arrived from almost outer-space...and was on a hat-trick!

Could he take three wickets in three balls? He'd never done it before!

He just wished that Mr Mason, the school cricket coach, could see him now...in his moment of possible glory!

The outcoming batsman, a young boy from Pillo called Samuel (in fact a neighbour of Jonathan and Jane) was determined to put a halt to his team's sudden decline!

"You'll not get me out with your Upper World trickery!" he called jovially as he passed Jamie on his way to his wicket.

The crowd fell silent.

The young batsman stared up the pitch at Jamie and gritted his teeth.

He had a cunning plan!

He would watch the spinning ball like a hawk as it fizzled towards him through the air...and hit it out of the Cavern before it had chance to land on the pitch and do its mystical work!

Jamie once again tossed himself a catch, wrapped his fingers round the ball and trotted into bowl.

Could he take his *third* wicket and become the first player in *Aqua Crysta* to take three wickets in three balls?

He skipped past the umpire and bowled the ball with as much spin as his fingers could tweak.

Daniel's eyes were fixed on the missile as it spun hypnotically towards him. He *had* to hit it before it landed on the pitch to do its magic!

Yes, now was the moment!

As planned, he confidently took one...two paces down the pitch and swung his bat at the mystical, spinning orb of grass and bark.

But...he missed! Instead, the ball bounced on the crystal dust and spun sharply to the left...straight into the stumps! The bails flew into the air...as did the arms of all the Galdo supporters, accompanied by an enormous cheer!

Jamie had taken a hat-trick...with all three wickets clean-bowled!

Immediately, the Pillo captain, Rufus Tinn, in true sportsman-like fashion, ran onto the arena and presented Jamie with a special cricket hat made from plaited fern fronds.

"Well done, sir!" he announced. "And here is your hat! I believe that is the custom in your World! When you take three wickets in three balls, you receive a hat! That's why it's called a 'hat-trick'!

And you can have the ball, too, as a keepsake!"
"Sorry about that!" murmured Jamie modestly. "I just hope I haven't
spoiled your game. I suppose you can still win! You've got *fifteen*
more wickets left! Thanks for the hat and the ball. I will treasure
them forever!"
"You must teach us your skill sometime!" insisted Rufus, as Jamie
rather shyly nodded and made his way across the dusty arena to the
alcove where the Queen and the others had watched.
"If you were not a hero before, young man, you certainly are *now*!"
smiled Queen Venetia. "You have entertained my people well, but
come, all of you, we have matters to discuss!"

By now, the assembled Aqua Crystans in the alcove
had swollen to nine in number. As well as the Queen, Lepho, Jessica,
Jamie, Jonathan and Jane...George Chubb, the crystal-carver, and his
old friends Josephine and Jasper, had arrived...the trio who had fled to
Aqua Crysta after the terrible events of 1790.
The blond haired brother and sister were instantly recognisable from
Spook's magic at Midge Hall during the sunny, Upper World
afternoon...although the velvet breeches, pale yellow dress and buckled
shoes had gone, to be replaced by typical purple Crystan cloaks and
plaited sandals. They all appeared older, of course...as you'd expect
after a couple of centuries! But having lived in *Aqua Crysta*, they
seemed no older than young middle aged!
They sat around a rectangular table...the Queen
and Mayor of Pillo at its head, the log casket in front of the Mayor.
Josephine and Jasper, of course, were saddened by the sight of the
casket. They hadn't seen it for over two hundred Upper World years.
Tears welled in their eyes as Jasper fingered his carved name underneath
and grievous memories flooded back.
"But I cannot understand how it comes to have these bejewelled
bands of gold around it, and the clasp!" he said sadly. "I just wrapped
it in rope! It was a gift for my father. My first wood carving.

But that terrible day when our parents were murdered has haunted us ever since!"

The Queen poured bramble wine from a crystal decanter into nine matching goblets, and for a few moments the assembly just sat quietly, with the cheers from the cricket match echoing around the vast cavern.

Jessica stared at the casket and whispered to Jamie, "I've seen it before, you know!"

"Where?"

"When we were in the Littlebeck Valley yesterday afternoon, standing on the bridge where we'd found one of dad's clues. Remember? I was gazing into the stream's bubbling waters...and I could see pictures of Lepho holding it in his arms and welcoming Jonathan and Jane on the quayside at Galdo! That's when all this magic began!"

"And I saw you both running into a crystal carving of *The Hermitage* on a stall in Galdo's market-place!" whispered Jane.

"And later, at George Chubb's house," whispered Jonathan, "a crystal model of Midge Hall vanished off a shelf..!"

"And landed up in *my hands!*" gasped Jessica. "We thought it was treasure dad had hidden...until it changed into a couple of mugs..!"

"With chocolate coins inside!" added Jamie, licking his lips, and beginning to feel a little peckish, especially after his exploits on the cricket field!

Fortunately, trays of all kinds of food began to arrive at the table, mainly produced by the *Chief Cooks of the Realm,* Megan Magwitch of Torrent Lodge and Dill Stem of Middle Floss. Soon, everyone was tucking into old favourites such as roast chestnut fingers with dandelion sauce, acorn slices with fern frond and daisy dip...and Jamie's favourite, toadstool roast with fried heather tips!

But however much the assembled party would have liked to have carried on feasting and drinking, there was important business to be attended to...and it was Lepho, the Mayor of Pillo, who firmly rapped his goblet on the table and began the meeting.

"It is clear that Midge Hall, Spook the cat and this log casket are central to our puzzle!" the ginger bearded Lepho began. "Together with the reason for *Lumina's* alarm. Is there something happening in the forest above that is more than the usual trivial activities of fairies and demons on Midsummer Night? It is as though the worst of them all... a *Shym-ryn*...has, by some means, come into possession of what we all dread...!"

"What's that?" gasped Jessica.

Lepho looked grimly into her eyes, and spoke words that made the blood in her veins run cold.

"*Any* object, even a strand of hair, belonging to their mighty enemy...the greatest and most powerful wizard of them all...

...*Merlyn!!*"

Chapter 13

As Jessica and Jamie recounted the events of the afternoon and evening in the forest, the hearts and spirits of everyone gathered around the table plummeted, like boulders thrown into the depths of Lake Serentina!

It became crystal clear that if something as important and significant as Merlyn's dagger, *Verax*, had fallen into the hands of a *Shym-ryn*, then the consequences could be so unthinkable...so terrible...that their effects would be felt *throughout* the Upper World...not just within the forest that lay above *Aqua Crysta*!

Legend has it that if any *Shym-ryn* (and there are hundreds in England, one in each patch of woodland or forest) should come by anything belonging to Merlyn, then they will unite into the strongest force imaginable...their sole intention being to destroy the wizard and bring chaos and evil to the whole of England!

And, what is more, with Merlyn having apparently vanished... (remember, he had been helplessly trapped in an owl's body for years and years until Jessica had released him, just weeks ago)...the *Shym-ryn* had become emboldened!

Now was *their* chance to become the grand masters of sorcery and to assume magical supremacy over England!

And, if that came about, it would undoubtedly mean that the forces of Evil would triumph over the forces of Good!

Life in England *would never, ever be the same again*!

The gathering of nine around the rectangular table fell silent and all eyes gazed at the mysterious log casket.

What *was* its significance?

Why *had* it suddenly appeared?

Had it anything to do with the *Shym-ryn* and the greater magic going on in the Upper World?

Then, amazingly, as though the casket knew it had completely captured its audience and was at the centre of all their thoughts and attention, the most astonishing thing happened!

The gold bands and lock that enwrapped the log began to glow as if they were bedded in the red, fiery coals of a furnace! The emeralds, too, glowed and sparkled as if they had suddenly been transformed into rubies!

Then, before the astonished eyes, the log's metallic bonds began to dissolve into nothing, leaving stripes of the rough wood scorched and black where the gold had been. The smell of burning bark filled the air as the bewildered onlookers wondered what was going to happen next.

Lepho reached forward and nervously put his hands on the ancient cut log.

"At last!" he exclaimed excitedly. "We can now discover the casket's secret!"

Slowly, he lifted the warm, upper half...and revealed the contents that had been locked away and bound in gold until now...this special mo...!

"*Dodo*! It's *Dodo*!" shrieked Jessica, as her eyes fell upon what was nestled in the hollowed out log. "It's from *Dodo*! He's in trouble! He needs our help!"

For there, held within the carved nest of splintered oak, lined with rough tan coloured sacking, was a length of rusted chain, two chunks of pale green time-crystal and a pair of beautifully coloured, translucent crystalid wings.

Jessica had recognised the items instantly, and could almost hear the strange croaky, clicking voice of the lonely Gargoyle she had befriended on Christmas Eve in the fearsome caverns which lay beneath *Aqua Crysta*. The Gargoyle that had been cruelly mistreated in the vast quarries and left behind when the rest of his kind had travelled back in time through the crystal-tunnel.

The message in the log was clear.

It was Dodo's plea for help.

But how the secret contents came to be inside the log, which was then bound with gold was a mystery. Surely Dodo couldn't have sealed and locked the casket! It was as though there was some other unknown, magical force involved...one which had dissolved the gold and allowed the log to be opened at exactly the right time! Was it the same sorcery that had removed the crystal carving of Midge Hall from George Chubb's house into the hands of Jessica? Was it the same magician that had changed the seasons in the Littlebeck Valley, transformed the Hall back to 1790 and *Old Soulsyke* back to 1953?

Somehow, by means they could not understand, the party gathered around the table knew that there was some connection with the greater magic that was happening on this Midsummer Eve in the Upper World. They also knew that they had to respond to the message...this plea for help.

But time was of the essence!

The *Shym-ryn* were gathering!
They had to reach Dodo as soon as possible and discover the connection...but he was deep, deep below, in dangerous, rocky depths beneath the Floss Cavern, way beyond the *Cave of Torrents*.
The journey would be long and hazardous...but they were confident that *whoever* or *whatever* was behind all this sorcery would help them.
Magical assistance was on its way!
And they hadn't long to wait!

Meanwhile, beyond the rocky alcove, the cricket match was still being enjoyed by the cheering crowds sat on the terraces of the *Meeting Hall Cavern*. Pillo were now just a handful of runs away from victory despite Jamie's hat-trick for Galdo. They had recovered well and only lost another four wickets.
But it was just as another over of bowling was about to begin that every single Aqua Crystan in the crowd or on the cricket field suddenly froze...and listened...
There was a faint high-pitched whining, buzzing sound coming from beyond the mouth of the *Meeting Hall*...from the Floss Cavern itself.
A sound no one had ever heard before.
And it was gradually becoming louder...!
...and louder!
Spectators began to stand and gaze around the vast cavern, mumbling to one another and gathering together their hats and cloaks and picnic bags. Happy, care-free smiles turned to puzzled, anxious frowns. Younger Crystans hid behind the cloaks of their mothers and fathers and peered up into the forest of glistening white and pink stalactites way above them, worry suddenly etched on their fresh faces. The cricketers, as calmly as possible, made their way from the exposed middle of the arena and joined their families around the edge. Aqua Crystans didn't know how to panic...they've never had to...but now, a strange, new sensation was just beginning to sweep through everyone. Hearts were thudding in chests, beads of

sweat were budding on foreheads, shivers were dancing along backbones.

Fear had struck in a moment!

Something was out there!

And worse still, the whole population of *Aqua Crysta* was gathered in *one place*!!

Suddenly, the whining and the buzzing became even louder!

Surely not the *Shym-ryn*!

Come to put an end to the time-less, magical kingdom!

Speculation and anxiety began to stir the crowd even more.

People began running from the terraces into the deep recesses of the cavern. Some were tripping, scrambling over one another. The young were swept up into arms, the old helped over the banks of terraces. The colourful rainbow of seated Aqua Crystans quickly dissolved into white as row upon row was deserted. The dark nooks and crannies became full to bursting and each mighty stalagmite sheltered dozens more.

The nine in the rocky alcove remained as calm as they could...

Queen Venetia and Lepho were powerless to do anything. They just had to watch and wait along with everyone else, terrifying thoughts racing through their heads...of disaster, catastrophe...and extinction!

Then...it happened!

The nightmare bit even harder.

Fear became *terror*!

The noise reached a climactic, crushing crescendo, forcing hands to cover ears...as the *something* appeared...in the mouth of the cavern!

One...two...three...four...five...devilishly hideous, black, flying creatures!

Frenzied screams instantly shrilled and echoed around the *Meeting Hall* as the cowering Aqua Crystans set eyes on the monstrous, bat-like squadron from the depths of the underworld.

Each one was at least half as long as the *Goldcrest*...all shiny black and tapering from a bulbous head with enormous eyes and fearsome pointed

beak to a slim tail armed with some kind of pincers. Hundreds of legs
dangled below each creature as they were kept aloft by quivering,
delicate, translucent wings.

What were they?

Where had they come from?

What were they looking for?

Shelter? Food? Slaves?

Jessica and Jamie looked at one another. They knew
exactly what the beasts were! The crystalids from the Forest Cellar!
In their ugly, black form they must have scurried down the *Harvest*
Passageway and emerged into the Larder Cave...and then flown down
the Floss Cavern. And, of course, because they didn't come down the
well, they were still the same size as they were in the Upper World!
The children felt suddenly guilty of bringing this havoc and chaos into
the tranquil world of *Aqua Crysta*.

The last time they'd seen the creatures, they had certainly been horrific,
but at least their size had been manageable!

Now, swooping and diving around the cavern, they were like a buzzing,
whining group of small, single-seater aeroplanes at an air-display!

And still, Jessica and Jamie kept asking themselves...why weren't they
like the crystalids they'd seen at Christmas? Beautifully coloured, like a
cross between a dragonfly and a humming bird? Perhaps this was just
some stage that all crystalids went through while changing from an egg
to a caterpillar to an adult!

"We've brought this horror here!" gasped Jessica to her brother. "Just
look at all the people! They're absolutely petrified! We've got to do
something! Are you with me?"

Jamie nodded, wondering what on earth his sister had in mind.

Suddenly, Jessica took his hand and they both walked
boldly from the alcove into the great, open arena.

"Come back! Come back!" shouted Lepho, Jonathan and Jane
desperately. "The creatures will..."

Queen Venetia cut them short.

"Fear not, my friends," she said calmly. "The magic is with them. I know they are safe!"

The two children walked defiantly on.

Soon they were well away from the alcove, and already, Aqua Crystans were watching them and pointing in astonishment.

Their panic-stricken yells and screams began to fade as they gazed at the two heroes marching bravely towards the centre of the arena.

Then a hush fell upon the crowd as the flying, menacing beasts circled and hovered directly above the two tiny figures.

The helpless prey was ready for the taking!

The buzzing and whining stopped.

The *Meeting Hall Cavern* was silent.

Five pairs of shining, jet black eyes stared unblinkingly down at the yellow and blue morsels beneath them!

The crowd held its breath along with Lepho, Jonathan and Jane!

Even the Queen looked worried!

Was this...the beginning...*of the end*??

Chapter 14

Without any warning, a sound like gunshot split the warm, silent air. The crowd cowered as one, all eyes still intently glued to the drama unfolding in the middle of the empty, crystal dust arena. Jessica and Jamie felt their knees suddenly tremble as they gazed up at the monsters hovering above them...their quivering, glassy wings almost a blurr.

Another shot suddenly rang out...then another, like whip lashes!
Crack! Crack!
Then...and everyone noticed it happening at the same time...
...jagged lines of colour, like forks of lightning in a night sky, began to split the jet black, shiny skins of the flying creatures...
Huge, long plates of black tore themselves off the bodies and fell away. Jessica and Jamie dived to the ground, covering their heads as more and more flakes of thick, smooth, almost metallic skin rained down on them. The transformation was incredible!

Within moments, the horrific animals had become the stunningly beautiful, gently hovering, dragonfly humming-birds of

Jessica's memory...if somewhat larger! Even the vicious tail pincers were discarded along with the waves of hundreds of short, scurrying legs. Now, six long, slender legs dangled down beneath each crystalid...greeny blue in colour to match their long, probing antennae that had sprouted from their rainbow heads.

Not only were the colours along the whole lengths of the bodies magnificent, but it was the way they were constantly changing against some kind of inner glow that made their audience gasp in admiration. They seemed to be made from transparent crystal of every shade of turquoise, amber, indigo and violet.

Thankfully, too, the menacing angry eyes had vanished to be replaced by eyes which almost seemed to smile, giving the faces a friendly look as though the creatures appreciated being admired!

Slowly but surely, the people emerged from their hiding places and watched as Jessica and Jamie stood up among the black, scaly debris. They both put their arms out in front of them in a gesture of friendship...and, amazingly...the giant crystalids began to hover downwards and land on the floor of the arena like five crystal winged helicopters! As each noiselessly touched down, clouds of crystal dust billowed up and swirled around the children's feet.

Jessica walked up to one, stood on her tip-toes, reached out a hand and stroked it on the head between its antennae...each one as long as Jessica was tall!

The crowd gasped and the Queen smiled.

Good fortune seemed to have arrived!

Without a word, the watching Aqua Crystans returned to their seats, unable to divert their gaze from the two children...Jessica especially, with her crown of rainbow feathers sprouting from her flowery scrunchie, somehow matching the crystalids!

Jamie stroked another of the giant insects, and then both of them beckoned Jonathan, Jane and Lepho to gently come forward and meet the new arrivals. The encounter was wonderfully magical and accompanied by whispers of amazement sweeping around the *Meeting*

Hall terraces. And when the strange creatures suddenly lowered their long, tapering bodies to the ground, the collective gasp of all the spectators was as if the cavern itself had just taken a breath!

Queen Venetia gracefully stepped forward and the audience fell silent again. She walked slowly into the midst of the magic and gently stroked each of the crystalids in turn.

The onlookers were spellbound!

After all, here was their Queen standing among creatures that only moments before had created such panic and pandemonium, and seemed to threaten their very existence!

But now, tranquility prevailed and a feeling of calm cloaked the watching Aqua Crystans. The crystalids were still and relaxed.

Their glassy wings were at rest. They seemed to be almost enjoying the attention.

It was then that Queen Venetia whispered to her five loyal and brave friends around her.

"These words are for you alone," she began. "Tell me, when I have finished, whether or not you can face the perils that lie ahead. The decision is yours!"

She paused and looked into the eyes of each of the five who had been the saviours of her Kingdom in the past.

"The magic is with us!" she smiled knowingly. "These enchanting creatures have been sent to help!"

Jessica and Jamie looked at one another, as did Jonathan and Jane.

What was coming next?

How could these fragile, crystal insects possibly help?

The Queen took Jessica's hand.

The words she whispered next set the heartbeats of her listeners racing.

"They will take you, speedily and safely, to your friend, Dodo...and to the magician who has brought you here. They are in one and the same place and in the gravest danger! It is the magician who will resolve the perils of the Upper World and see that Good triumphs over Evil!

Will you take on the task?"

The Queen looked again at each of her warriors.

"You mean...we have to...*fly?*" gasped Jessica, a mixture of alarming and thrilling thoughts flashing through her imagination at once.

"But what if..."

"Like this, sis!"

Already, Jamie had scrambled aboard his crystalid, his mind made up! And there he was, lying face down on top of its crystal body...

...his knees gripping its sides and his hands grasping the lowest, thickest parts of its two antennae.

"*Sabre* will have me there in next to no time!" he called, as the crowd burst into applause, suddenly aware of what was going on!

Jessica could resist no longer.

"And *Rudolph* will take *me*!" she beamed as she clambered onto her crystal steed.

A moment later, The Queen had her answer.

Tears welled in her eyes.

All five of her heroes had scrambled aboard their flying machines, ready and willing to face the perils ahead.

The watching Aqua Crystans rose to their feet and cheered, as the five mounted crystalids lifted their slender bodies from the crystal dust of the arena. They seemed as calm as ever, not in the least concerned about having passengers clinging to their backs nor about the noise that filled the cavern! Each one just stood there on its six fragile legs, wings beginning to quiver, seemingly without a care in the world!

"Ready for lift off, folks?" called Jamie, all set for the ride of his life-time.

"Seat belts fastened?" called Jessica, as *Rudolph's* wings began to quiver faster and faster behind her.

"Good fortune to you all!" beamed the Queen. "May the magic be with you!"

"Our latest Quest will meet with the same success as those that have gone before!" gasped Lepho, the Mayor of Pillo, from his rather undignified position on top of *Icarus*. "Of that, I have no doubt!"

The wings of all five crystalids began to flutter faster and faster until a gentle hum and then a buzz drowned the sound of the cheering and clapping from the terraces.

"Goodbye, your Majesty!" shouted Jonathan above the din from *Lancelot's* wings, his dark hair ruffled by the breeze.

"We'll soon have even more to celebrate!" added Jane aboard *Guinevere*, her pigtails bobbing up and down.

"Goodbye, my children!" mouthed the Queen, unable to compete with the sounds of imminent take-off. "Goodbye and good fortune!"

With that, the beautiful, crystal flying machines lifted themselves from the arena amid another gasp of wonder by the crowd. They hovered and spun slowly until all five were facing the vast open mouth of the cavern...Jessica's *Rudolph* in front and then *Icarus* and *Sabre* followed by *Lancelot* and *Guinevere*. Then, with a slight dip forward, as though they were bowing to the Queen, the amazing aerial display team glided over the arena, through the mouth and into the Floss Cavern. All the riders would have loved to wave to the crowds but they were all grimly hanging on to the antennae, their hearts pounding in their chests! They couldn't escape from thoughts of slipping off and plunging into the River Floss, or the wings clipping the rocky sides of the cavern or hitting an overhanging stalactite!

But they needn't have worried, as it soon became clear that the journey...or *the flight*...was going to be smooth and trouble-free! These creatures certainly knew how to fly! Even with passengers clinging on their backs!

In no time at all, the rainbow squadron was flying past the pair of thin, dangling ropes that swayed and arced down from the mists at the bottom of the well to the white, pebbly shore of the Floss.

Jessica and Jamie had scarcely time to think about their everyday world that lay way above them at the top of the well's iron rungs...or their father, still asleep in *Deer Leap*! They just gazed through squinted eyes at the magnificent beauty all around them that was zooming by! Their trips on the *Goldcrest* had been pretty swift! But this was a completely different kettle of fish! It was more like being strapped to a low flying jet, as the crystalids swerved and banked, cutting like knives through the warm, sweet smelling air!

Moments later, they flew past the Larder Steps and then the deserted village of Middle Floss perched like a swallow's nest high above the Floss. The Narrows came next where the crystalids had to fly in single file...and then the junction of the Floss Cavern and the *Cave of Torrents*. How the crystalids knew to turn right was a mystery to everyone, but turn right they did, swooping over Knapweed's crystal grinding mill and into the much lower and narrower cave.

One after the other, the shallow torrent steps swept by beneath the whirring wings, like a never-ending staircase of rushing, bubbling water. Torrent Lodge flashed by in a second, instantly tickling Jamie's taste buds as he imagined all the scrumptious delicacies produced by Megan Magwitch and her daughters! Jessica traced the narrow path that wound through the cave hugging the stream...it had seemed such a long, long trek when they'd walked the whole length of it on Christmas Eve! But now it was quickly unwinding beneath her like a darting, wriggling snake!

Soon they would be at the cave's end, with its last and highest

'THE CAVE OF TORRENTS'

waterfall...but what was going to happen next?

Every rider knew that beyond the last torrent was a steep flight of steps, a balcony and then the narrow passage which lead to the *Star Chamber*! The crystalids were too large to get through!

The amazing flight was surely coming to an end!

But as everyone hung on as tightly as they could, the creatures began to fly even faster...and faster! Suddenly, the last torrent came into view and Jessica's *Rudolph* swooped upwards. He was heading not to the passageway but to the top of the falls! Closer and closer he flew, followed by the others...until, in a moment, the warm, comforting, crystal light of *Aqua Crysta* was extinguished.

'THE LAST TORRENT'

They had left the magical Kingdom behind and entered unknown territory! A dark, gloomy cavern stretched ahead, lit only by the faint greeny glow from the crystalids themselves. Here, there were no glinting crystals embedded in white walls, nor ceilings packed with pink stalactites. Instead, dull brown, gritty rock was everywhere, without a hint of light, except the crystalid glow reflected in the fast flowing stream below. It reminded Jessica and Jamie of the caves they had scrambled through beyond the *Star Chamber* when they had been following the Gargoyles down to their quarry.

Onwards they flew, following the water, until the riders saw ahead of them a great shaft of red light beaming upwards from some kind of opening in the cave floor. The cave began to widen into a cavern, the stream looping to the left of the ever growing column of fiery light. As they approached the almost solid beam, the crystalids began to fly slower and slower, until they were just hovering. It was as if they were anxious about flying into the beam itself...although they could have easily flown around it, following the stream.

One by one, the five crystalids pushed their heads into the red light, their passengers squinting in the brightness.

Slowly but surely, the flying creatures inched forwards until all five were hovering above the great gaping hole in the cavern floor.

The riders gazed downwards...and it was then that they all suddenly knew exactly where they were! They were above a hole in the roof of the *Star Chamber*! They could just about make out the forest of red stalagmites soaring from its floor...way, way below. They could even see a couple of the five cave entrances which lead from the vast, fiery cavern's floor like the spokes of a giant wheel. One of them had lead to the Gargoyles' quarry on Christmas Eve. And one had lead to the staircase, at the foot of which the evil, plotting Tregarth had met his savage end in the jaws of *Gargon,* the monster of the underworld.

Then, as the crystalids hovered above the great hole, a strange, eerie sound began to creep up from below. It was as though the red beam of light itself was humming its own ghostly tune. Humming mixed with whining...a sound that, somehow, seemed familiar to Jessica and Jamie.

They looked anxiously at one another from the backs of *Rudolph* and *Sabre*.

The sound grew louder and louder...and, at the same time, more threatening and haunting!

The crystalids began to hover slightly less smoothly, a little more jerkily!

Tension and worry was sweeping through the crystal steeds as well as their riders!

Something was down there!

The question was...*what*??

Chapter 15

It wasn't long before the first signs of movement could be seen...far, far, below...in the fiery depths of the enormous *Star Chamber*. Among the glowing, towering stalagmites, a host of twinkling, fluttering points of light suddenly appeared. They swirled and curled around the red towers like grains of glistening sand caught and tossed in a whirlwind. Then they seemed to merge and move together in unison, as one great, twisting stream of light particles, like a shoal of tiny fish or a cloud of starlings. Its iridescence constantly changed, sweeping from turquoise and amber, melting into blues and greens, and back again.

It was a beautiful, mesmerising display and almost sent its aerial observers into trances...especially when the hypnotic, lightly buzzing swarm began to weave upwards like some kind of serpent from a snake-charmer's basket. On and on, higher and higher, it unwound from the floor of the cavern...as more and more points of light seemed to gush in from the five cave mouths around the floor.

The heartbeats of the riders began to race as the headless, spiralling serpent approached the hole in the roof.

To be honest, none of them was quite sure what to make of it!

On the one hand, the incredibly enticing spectacle seemed to be...well, just that! A wonderfully magical sight to enjoy! But on the other hand, a possibly threatening swarm of...

It was at that moment that Jamie suddenly called out above the growing din, almost losing grip of *Sabre's* antennae,

"They're *crystalids*! Hundreds and thousands of them!"

As the first tiny creatures fluttered through the hole and inquisitively inspected their giant relatives, everyone grinned with amazement, fears dismissed in an instant!

The insect hosts from below were all perfect miniatures of their guests, no larger than dragonflies...and, within seconds, virtually all of them had swarmed through the hole into the cavern, filling it with even more light!

They were absolutely everywhere! The air was thick with them, all landing and taking off from the bodies of the giant crystalids and their riders! There was no point in swatting them away, there was just so many of them! Literally thousands and thousands! Remarkably, dozens of them were carrying bundles of sticky crystal dust at the end of their long beaks...and were actually feeding their giant cousins while they hovered. Jessica watched in amazement as one after another hovered at the end of *Rudolph's* beak, like humming birds by a tropical flower. Each time, her giant steed's green tongue would shoot out and wrap itself around a crystal bundle and whip it into its beak!

After all the feeding seemed to have finished, the huge swarm began to quieten and hover around the guests. There was just the sound of the stream and the gentle hum of thousands of pairs of fluttering wings.

Then, all at once, the antennae of all five giants began to quiver, and a peculiar, high-pitched, vibrating noise filled the air. The riders, who were still gripping the antennae, began vibrating too! So much so that they had to loosen their grips! The noise began to change tone, then stop and start again! Different notes...some long, some short, some high, some low...echoed around the cavern. It was as though the giant visitors were singing!

"They're *talking*!" gasped Lepho from the back of *Icarus*. "They are actually *communicating* with the swarm! It's incredible!"

Then the giants fell silent.

The notes faded away.

Just the gurgling waters below could be heard.

"What's going to happen next?" whispered Jane from *Guinevere*.

"Well, we've all been re-fuelled!" suggested her brother with a grin. "Perhaps we're ready for take-off again!"

But what *did* happen next nearly caused all five riders to topple from their steeds in astonishment!

The swarm began to answer back!

All of them, thousands at once, with exactly the same series of musical notes...like an enormous insect choir! The cavern and the red beam of light were filled to the brim with a beautifully musical succession of notes and tones. The riders gazed around them in utter wonder!

Then *that* message, whatever it was, stopped...and the giants replied...again in perfect unison and harmony!

The host of hovering dragonflies burst forth once more...and then the musical interlude ended as suddenly as it had begun.

Whatever had been said...had been said!

The dialogue between hosts and guests was over, its contents a total mystery to the Aqua Crystans and Jessica and Jamie.

The quivering antennae of the giants stopped dead and the riders resumed their grips. A moment later, the glassy wings began to flutter more strongly and the huge crystalids crept through the air across the bright beam of red.

The second part of the flight was about to begin!

To where, none of the riders knew!

The destination was only known to the crystalids and the magician who was conjuring all this enchantment.

To Queen Venetia's intrepid adventurers, the magic was beckoning them forwards. It was not an endeavour for faint hearts, and there was definitely no turning back!

Whatever lay ahead had to be faced!

The deed had to be done!

Shortly afterwards, the warm, red light above the *Star Chamber* and the swarm of friendly crystalids had been left far behind. The journey through the gloomy cavern had resumed, with just the babbling stream for company. On and on the five giant dragonflies flew with their passengers clinging on to their antennae.

The cavern gradually became cooler and damp...and larger and larger. They passed several dark cave mouths to the left and right, but the flying creatures seemed to know exactly where they were going... straight ahead!!

The stream below maintained its width and vigour for a while, but, then it, too, became increasingly wide and faster flowing.

The riders could also sense a damp, earthy, soily odour in the air.

It reminded Jessica and Jamie of the smell in the Harvest Passageway as it neared its exit in the Forest. The smell of the Upper World!

Surely this cavern couldn't lead to somewhere up there, as well!

Mile upon mile they seemed to fly...the scents of woodland becoming stronger and stronger, the stream constantly with them. But just as the riders were beginning to think they would suddenly emerge into some moonlit, wooded valley in the Upper World...they began to see, in the dim crystal light cast by the crystalids...unexpected objects littering the banks of the stream!

Lengths of rusted chain, pick-axes...then one, two, three, four upturned wagons, some with wooden wheels, some without.

Bits of torn sacking were scattered everywhere amid branches of trees, metal pots, spades...all sprinkled with twinkling, dead crystalids.

And then, more gruesomely...the body of an enormous, unmoving stony Gargoyle, partly submerged in the fast, flowing stream! Alarm bells began to ring in the ears of the riders!

Memories of the Gargoyles' horrific kingdom beneath *Aqua Crysta* flooded into their minds!

But this time, of course, everything was huge! Last time, at Christmas, they'd gone down the misty staircase which had made them Upper World size. Now a single chain link was as big as Lepho, and the wagons the size of *Deer Leap*! The Gargoyle was the size of the great white soldier they'd seen by the top of the well the Summer before, its hands the size of removal vans at least!!

But why were all these things from their abandoned realm *here*, miles away? Not to mention the remains of a dead Gargoyle?

Suddenly, ahead of them, to the right, was another cave entrance...bigger than any of the others they had seen.

More and more of the debris was scattered around its mouth...even piles of the stuff! And there were two more gigantic, mountainous bodies of Gargoyles, almost as fearsome dead as they were alive!

Then, as the squadron of crystalids approached the dark, menacing gaping hole in the cavern's side, all the riders noticed movement among a great drift of coiled, rusty chains!

An arm! A Gargoyle arm was moving, its solid stone muscles flexing in the dull light. Its three scaly fingers and thumb, each tipped with stone claws, were scraping at the wet rocks and gravel at the edge of the stream, like some monstrous mechanical digger!

"It has to be *Dodo*!" cried Jessica. "He's injured or trapped!"

"But what can we do?" yelled Jamie, against the increasing roar of the stream.

The crystalids flew closer and closer.

More and more of the Gargoyle came into view.

A vast shoulder like a hillside, his great swathe of sculpted, concrete like hair on a head pushed into the gravel, face down. Beyond, stretching into the darkness of the cave was his upper body, then his legs.

Rudolph and the rest of the crystalids flew down the length of the Gargoyle, their passengers gazing downwards at the vast body of the sprawling giant.

Then suddenly, they heard it!

A rumbling, thunderous growl from just ahead!

The crystalids halted and hovered.

Their passengers stared into the gloom.

Another fearsome growl shook the air!

The crystalids began to glow brighter than ever they had glowed before.

Perhaps a sign of fear!

A soft amber light filled the cave...

...and unveiled before them...a sight of such horror...that the riders' blood froze in their veins and their mouths fell open, speechless with terror!!

There...almost within touching distance...was the colossal open jaw of a creature from prehistory, its jagged teeth clamped viciously onto the ankles and feet of the poor Gargoyle!

Above the teeth were two flaring, black nostrils and then two half closed, bulbous eyes. All were set in the ferocious, scaly head of a reptile of such magnitude, it could have been a Tyrannosaurus Rex itself!!

It was undoubtedly *Gargon*...the fearsome creature of the underworld that had terrorized the Gargoyles and killed the treacherous Tregarth.

Jamie and Jonathan had seen the monster before, of course, when its long, lashing tongue had nearly wrapped itself round their legs in the passage beyond the last torrent. But here it was again...menacingly crouched in its dark lair, its helpless victim gripped in its vice-like jaws.

Dodo had to be rescued...but how? And to what danger to the riders and their crystalids? For the moment it was stalemate.

Gargon was lying there like a great dog...growling, with a bone clenched between its teeth, refusing to let it go. If the reptile released the Gargoyle then it knew it could be in peril itself at the hands of its former prey. But then again, the Gargoyle was weak. He had been dragged from near the *Star Chamber* up into the monster's den, unable to struggle free from the creature's grip. Now *Dodo* was exhausted, his energy seemingly spent. He tried to pull his feet from the jaws of his captor, but to no avail. He was well and truly trapped.

Equally, neither the crystalids nor their riders could do anything! They just stared into the amber glinting eyes of the monster, and felt sympathy for *Dodo*. But the riders knew in their hearts that they had a hidden, secret strength. They felt close to their goal, and they knew the magic would come to their aid. Surely it hadn't guided them all the way here...for nothing!

They watched and waited, hovering in front of the gigantic, snarling head, fearful but resolute. The rows of ominous teeth before them could threaten as much evil as they wanted, but they would remain steadfast and bold!

But where *was* the magic?

Would it *ever* come?

Suddenly, the antennae of the crystalids began to vibrate! The delicate flying creatures looked at one another and then those peculiar, musical notes began to fill the monster's lair. The reptile's bulbous eyes widened, showing slit-like, black pupils set in orange irises. It sensed that something was about to happen!

The stalemate was about to be broken!

The notes became louder. Some long, some short, all in different tones. A message was being sent!

But to whom?

The music stopped.

Silence.

Then in the far, far distance...way back in the cavern behind them...everyone heard the gentle reply!

Soft musical notes drifted on the air...some long, some short, all in different tones! Help was coming!

Gargon shifted unconfortably on its great, clawed front feet.

Its eyes blinked, with a certain anxiety about them.

But still, its jaws were unyielding, clamped on its victim.

Dodo tried to turn his face out of the gravel, and summon every muscle and sinew in his legs and arms to help free himself.

But still, he remained stuck fast.

The riders looked at one another, wondering what on earth was going to happen next!

And a second later it happened!

A *new* monster had arrived!

And its size was absolutely *awesome*!

Chapter 16

The ever-changing, iridescent cloud that swirled into the cavern from the *Star Chamber* was like a vast, glistening, tidal wave of oiled water. Along with its incessant, high-pitched, whining hum, the great headless form rolled towards *Gorgon's* den with majestic grace. Each individual, tiny element of the whole couldn't be made out...but together, they made an unstoppable, invincible force!

Within seconds, the five giant crystalids, their riders and the enormous reptilian head were swamped by thousands of whirling, buzzing dragonflies. *Rudolph* and the rest withdrew and watched from above the stream. They would let their miniature cousins do the deed!

The air became a thick, crystalid soup...and although they had no power to sting nor bite, the pure effect of their noise and colour...and above all, their numbers...had the desired result!

The battle was a short one. At first, *Gorgon* resisted and held on to its prey, but then, with crystalids filling its nostrils and choking its throat...the great gaping jaws opened like those of a huge crocodile. In a trice *Dodo* was free and, with a burst of energy, pulled himself forwards and into the stream. The monstrous reptile reared up on its short front legs, swung its head wildly, snapping its jaws ferociously. The five hovering crystalids quickly glided backwards, taking themselves and their riders out of danger.

Hundreds of crystalids were crushed and swallowed, but it had no effect on the determination of the whole army. On and on, they swarmed around the beast's head until it could hardly breathe.

Then with one last vain lunge at *Dodo,* it dragged its gigantic body out of its lair and headed back down the main cavern, roaring savagely as it went, its great swaying tail swishing into the pursuing cloud of crystalids. Many more of the brave, tiny warriors perished...but the immense, united force had won the day!

Gorgon had been defeated!

Dodo had been rescued!

The Gargoyle pulled his body out of the water and sat on the shore amid the debris his captor had collected over the years. The giant crystalids hovered around his huge head, his face now recognisable to all the riders as *Dodo* - the one remaining Gargoyle, left behind when his compatriots had vanished into the past through the crystal time-tunnel. The Gargoyle who had befriended Jessica and caused mayhem on Sandsend beach and at the railway station on that Summer's day in 1954!

There was no doubt about his gratitude! He jabbered away in his clicketty language and a beam of a smile illuminated his stony face. He put out his great hand and the five crystalids in turn landed on his rocky palm. Everyone dismounted and stood between the curved fingers looking up at the massive, smiling face!

"Well, *that* was *some* battle!!" gasped Jamie, wielding his imaginary sword.

"It was indeed!" agreed Lepho, brushing himself down and stretching his legs. "But we *still* have matters to attend to!"

Jonathan and Jane patted *Lancelot* and *Guinevere*.

"Somewhere nearby, there should be a magician!" said Jonathan, gazing into the vastness of the dark cavern.

"But where?" asked his sister.

It was then that they all noticed Jessica, leaning on *Dodo's* thumb, and staring into the blackness of the main cavern further upstream.

"What's up, sis?" asked Jamie. "Can you see something?"

Jessica pointed into the gloom.

They all looked.

In the dim light they could just about see something stretching into the distance, partly in the rushing water, partly on the shore.

Something white.

A ruined building perhaps...with great, long, white, rounded beams leading to a series of immense white arches.

As they squinted into the darkness, Jane suddenly screamed.

"Look, look!" she yelled, pointing to the left and right. "Feet!"

"Bones of feet!" shouted Jamie. "See the toes at the top!"

"It's a *skeleton*!!" exclaimed Jessica. "And it's as big as *Dodo*!"

The Gargoyle lowered his hand to the shore and the five explorers clambered over a twisted pile of giant, rusted chain links. Jamie reached one of the feet first.

It was easily as high as *Deer Leap*!

Its heel bone was half buried in the gravel, its toe bones like the battlements of a castle tower.

They scrambled alongside the immense fibula bone of the lower leg, which swelled in thickness up to the bulging knee. Then came the femur bone which lead to the gigantic pelvic girdle and the great hip bones. Sagging between the hips was an enormous bridge of brown, as wide as a country lane, with a massive rectangular framework of decorated gold halfway along. The bridge dipped beyond the hips and swept beneath the skeleton to make a complete circle.

"It's a belt!" exclaimed Jessica, with a look of horror on her face.

"And we've seen it before! All of us have!"

They all looked at one another.

"You mean to say that its the same skeleton we saw in the alchemist's room at the *Golden Waters of Needle Crag* just a few weeks ago?" gasped Jamie.

Jessica nodded and Lepho agreed.

"It *must* be Lucius!" he whispered, scratching his stubbly, ginger chin. "Or rather his skeleton!"

"But what's it doing *here*?" wondered Jane.

"We're miles away from *Needle Crag*!"

The party walked on, gazing around in astonishment.

A moment later they were all under the huge white arches that made the rib-cage. As they stood next to the thick spine with all its vertebrae, it felt like being inside some enormous cathedral of bone!

Dangling from some of the ribs were raggy remnants of brown material...the remains of the gown Lucius was wearing when he had poisoned himself.

They were all now convinced that it was definitely the skeleton of the alchemist who had lived at the *Golden Waters* and taken his own life when he had turned the wise and good wizard Merlyn into an owl!

But surely they hadn't come all this way to meet a *dead* magician! Surely this wasn't the end of the magic!

It was just at that very moment, as doubts and uncertainties were beginning to enter all their minds, when a totally unexpected sound rose above the din of the stream. A sound that at once filled the tiny explorers with both fear and wonder.

It was a voice!

A voice that filled every nook and cranny of the cavern.

But a voice of warmth and welcome.

Everyone looked at one another in amazement!

It couldn't be the skeleton!

They looked back at *Dodo*!

It certainly wasn't him!

"Thankyou...all of you...from the depths of my heart!"

The words were spoken by a man in deep, commanding tones but ones which were friendly, almost affectionate. From a man of peace and goodwill.

But where were the words coming from?

There was no sign of anyone!

"I have long been expecting you...Jessica, Jamie, Jonathan, Jane and Lepho...Queen Venetia's five loyal heroes...brought here in all haste by the courageous, winged crystalids. Their deed is now complete and fulfilled. They must return to either *Aqua Crysta*, by the way they have come, or venture down into the underworld to become kings and queens among their kind. I thank them for their endeavours."

As though mystically commanded, the five giant crystalids hovered slowly into the air above *Dodo's* clawed hand, majestically bowed toward their riders...and then turned and flew back down the cavern. Their colourful light faded into the dark distance until they were just tiny specks...and then they vanished altogether. The hearts of their riders sank. In a short time, the crystalids had become good friends...and they hadn't even been able to say a proper 'goodbye'.

Tears welled in their eyes. Would they ever see them again?

Without the soft light from their crystal bodies, the cavern was plunged into darkness. But as the eyes of the intrepid travellers adjusted, they all noticed a new green glow illuminating the cavern walls, the stream, *Dodo* and the enormous skeleton.

They gazed up into the chilling, archway of ribs that enfolded them and then along the spine towards the gleaming skull.

It was then that they noticed the source of the new light!

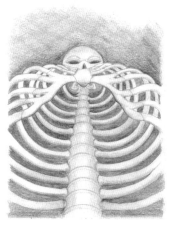

Hovering in the dark, just beyond the skull, were two green discs, each split down the centre by a slender streak of black, shaped like a willow leaf. The glistening emeralds were the size and shape of a pair of Roman soldiers' shields, but glassy and shiny...with clear, watery depths marbled with merging tones of flowing, liquid green, like sunlit coral pools. Jessica almost expected a shoal of brightly coloured tropical fish or a turtle to dart across them at any moment!!

Suddenly, the voice spoke again.

It was coming from the hypnotic discs.

"You have saved your friend, *Dodo*, from his captor...but you have also saved *me...Lucius*...alchemist, magician and, at one time, both rival and friend of the great wizard, *Merlyn!*"

Jessica and Jamie looked at one another in disbelief.

"But you are *dead!*" called out Jessica. "The wise sisters of *Needle Crag*, and your beloved Grizelda, told us so!"

"You poisoned yourself!" insisted Jamie, above the roar of the stream. "We saw your skeleton in your cellar above the *Golden Waters!*"

The emerald discs suddenly widened and moved closer.

More green light flooded the cavern...and what the five explorers saw before them made them gasp as one!

The discs were a pair of eyes!

A pair of eyes set within a face of pure white fur adorned with white whiskers and a pale, pinkisk nose!

A cat's face!

A living cat's face!

And it was coming closer...

and closer...

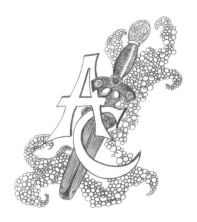

Chapter 17

As the snowy white face moved closer and closer to the great dome of the skull, the bewildered travellers suddenly pelted across the cavern floor and hid behind the massive ribs! After all, celebrated warriors or not, they were *tiny*... no bigger than baby mice...a mere mouthful, a titbit for a hungry cat!

Then, when the face was next to the skull, they could just make out the vast white body that followed behind...and its great serpent of a tail, twitching in the...

"It's *Spook*!!" Jessica exclaimed.

"It's *Spook* again! He's been...or she's been...with us ever since yesterday afternoon...at the bridge next to Midge Hall!"

"I'm a '*he*', if you please!" came the warm tones of the voice again.

And the voice was coming *from the cat*!

The cat was speaking!

It was the cat that had done all the talking!

The Aqua Crystans, together with Jessica and Jamie, were all equally shocked and confused! Slowly but confidently, they stepped out from behind their ribs.

"You mean you are *Spook*...and *Lucius*?" gasped Jamie.

"And *this* is your human skeleton?" burst Jane.

The cat nodded.

"I am indeed Lucius...and I have been in the body of a cat ever since I transformed Merlyn into an owl!" he admitted sadly. "But now that spell has been broken, I must return to my former self. Then I must travel to *Aqua Crysta* and be re-united with my beloved Grizelda and her beautiful mare, *Gabrielle!*"

"But the skeleton?" asked Jonathan.

"Magic, my son! Pure magic!" said the cat. "Although not *perfect magic*, I must admit! I tried to conjure my remains from *Needle Crag* to a place near *Aqua Crysta*. Then my plan was to transform myself from the cat you call *Spook* back into Lucius the alchemist and magician. I would climb down into your enchanted realm and..."

"But the place your skeleton arrived was...," Jane gasped.

"Yes, right here...next to *Gorgon's* lair!" the cat sadly admitted, shaking his head. "And, even worse! He was at home!"

"And if you changed back into a human-being here...!" burst Jessica, at last beginning to understand.

"...You'd be minced meat! A satisfying dinner-for-one!" finished Jamie.

"But how did you...as a cat...get here?" asked Jonathan.

Spook cast a glance backwards along the cavern.

"The well shaft up to Midge Hall is just a short walk away!"

"You mean this stream flows *under* Midge Hall," exclaimed Jessica, "and it leads to the *Cave of Torrents* in *Aqua Crysta*??"

"Of course it does, sis!" burst Jamie. "That's how the log casket got from Midge Hall to Torrent Lodge! Jasper chucked it down the well over two centuries ago...it floated downstream...got stuck in all this junk in *Gargon's* den...and then *Dodo* used it to get a message to *Aqua Crysta*..."

"But how come the log shrunk, so that a tiny Aqua Crystan could pick it up from the shore at Torrent Lodge...?" asked Jonathan.

"...And how come there were gold bands around it?" chipped in Jane.

"Now, now, now!" muttered Lepho at last, slightly sharply. "Questions, questions, questions! Those mysteries will be explained in time...but for the moment we *still* have work to do!!"

"And speaking of *time*!" added Jamie, staring at his watch. "It's started again! It's nearly five past three! It must be because we're not far from the Upper World!"

"In which case a plan has to be hatched!" said Lepho, looking intently at the rest of the party. "But first, Lucius must be allowed to resume his human form! I think we had better all stand back!"

The comforting voice of the cat once again filled the cavern.

"I agree, my friend! Then, once back to my old self, I will inform you of my plans to pay back my debt to Merlyn by ensuring the evil *Shym-ryn* are defeated!"

"You know about the *Shym-ryn*...and the dagger, *Verax*?" gasped Jessica, feeling pangs of guilt again.

"I do, indeed," replied the cat sadly, "and I know that they thirst for magical power over the Upper World! They long to wrestle supremacy from Merlyn...and now that they have *Verax* in their possession, there is great danger to us all! And worse still, Midsummer Night is upon us! This is the time they will seek victory!"

"But where and when?" burst Jamie.

"To those questions I think I have the answers, but first to the business of my transformation!"

With the onlookers well sheltered behind an upturned wagon just beyond the towering feet of the skeleton, the great cat closed his eyes. The cavern was plunged into blackness.

Nothing could be seen...but above the gurgling waters, the strange, meaningless words of spell could just be heard. Everyone knew they were in the midst of powerful magic! A supreme sorcerer was at work! The words were followed by even stranger sounds...murmurings, shufflings and even a screech almost like an owl! Then an explosion of brilliant white light lit the cavern and the surprised faces of everyone! Suddenly, the cat leaped forward from behind the skull and seemed to dissolve into the rib-cage!

Spook had gone! Probably never ever to be seen again!

Instead, the body of a man was beginning to form before the eyes of the astonished observers...lying on the shore, wrapped in a brown gown with a leather, golden buckled belt. Nearest to the amazed witnesses, the bony feet became black, shiny boots with the glinting heads of nails sparkling in the leather soles. Then the figure slowly sat up and looked around.

The face of the man was young and rosy cheeked, beneath a mane of long, raven black hair. His eyes, as you may have expected, were emerald green...and they cast the same soft light as they had done before.

"Where are you?" he gently asked.

Again, the warm voice was identical to that of the cat!

Lepho led the rest from their shelter and they made their way along the gravelly shore to the hand which beckoned them. They clambered on board and sat amid the fleshy fingers, one banded with a gold ring with an emerald stone. As they settled on the palm, a torrent of clicketty, clicks from *Dodo* suddenly crackled in the air.

The Gargoyle had sat quietly watching all the happenings with curiosity. Now he, too, wanted to know what was going to happen next!

When all were ready, Lucius spoke.

"My friends," he began, glancing into the eyes of his audience, one by one, "you have bravely completed your task. Your work is done and, in time, your endeavours will pass into legend and will be told and re-told by generations to come! Your part in the saving of the Upper World from evil will be celebrated through time eternal!"

Jessica and Jamie looked at one another...they'd never thought of themselves as *legends*!

"On the other hand, *my* work has yet to be completed," Lucius continued, looking determinedly at his listeners.

He paused, as if he was summoning strength from some unknown, magical source.

Then he spoke again.

"This is my plan!" he confidently announced, raising his audience towards his huge face.

"First, I want you all to follow me along the stream to Midge Hall. There, in the quiet of the Upper World, I will leave you and be swept away within a powerful spell to be re-united with Merlyn!

He is already at a place, the whereabouts of which I dare not say for fear of destroying the magic! But, believe me, it is a place where enchantments and sorcery have been practised for centuries. It is the cauldron of all magic! A place where magical supremacy is won and lost. The *Shym-ryn* are gathered there now, as I speak, dancing in the dawning sky and celebrating their possession of *Verax*! They will be taunting Merlyn and threatening his powers. Come, it is time I was by his side!"

With that, Lucius cupped his hands to secure his new friends and then, with a sudden urgency, made his way upstream along the cavern. *Dodo* followed, both giants having to bend almost double to avoid the low roof. Soon they were below the well-shaft that lead up to the old hall. The Gargoyle helped the magician up to the first iron rung, which he grasped with his free hand.

"My friends, you will be safe in the deep pocket of my cloak while I climb! Soon you will be back in the Littlebeck Valley amid the roar of its great waterfall!"

Moments later, the heroic travellers and the two giants were within the crumbling walls of Midge Hall, breathing in the sweet air. It was still dark, although there was just the merest hint of light streaking across the sky, dissolving the stars. The full moon was out of sight, somewhere below the trees, its silvering of the woodland over for another night. The only sound that could be heard was the never-ending, thunderous, tumbling rumble of the waterfall.

"There is no time to lose!" said Lucius, impatient to conjure his spell. He looked down at the tiny party gathered on his palm.

"*Dodo* will see you all safely back to the Harvest Passageway near the well beyond Old Soulsyke! It will take him about an hour depending upon his strength. You will soon be back in *Aqua Crysta* and then Jessica and Jamie can climb the well to return to Upper World dimensions. You will all be secure in his hands. Some creatures of the night may see the giant Gargoyle striding across the countryside, but there will be no humans about at this time!"

"Will we see you again?" asked Jane.

"You will indeed!" replied the magician. "After our battle is won, I fully intend to return and climb down the well into *Aqua Crysta* and live forever with my beloved Grizelda!"

So, with the Aqua Crystans and Jessica and Jamie safely cupped in *Dodo's* rough, stony hands, Lucius said farewell. The Gargoyle stepped out of the ruined hall and glanced back at the magician standing alone in the hollow room surrounded by fallen masonry and ancient wooden beams. The children peeped between *Dodo's* fingers and just about managed to wave a cheerful goodbye. "Good luck!" they called, but already Lucius was lost in his magic, conjuring up the words he needed to send him on his way.

As the Gargoyle ran along the narrow path above the valley, cradling his precious cargo, the sorcerer had completed his magical incantation. And by the time *Dodo* passed *The Hermitage,* Lucius had vanished.

Would his plan work?

Would Good triumph over Evil at the mysterious battle-site?

Only time would tell!

But one thing was certain.

Nothing would *ever* be the same again!

Meanwhile, just as *Dodo* was striding as quietly as he could through the shallow ford at Littlebeck hamlet, Mr Dawson's alarm rang out loudly at *Deer Leap*. Through one bleary eye he squinted at the offending clock and then silenced the unwelcome bell with a weary hand.

"Quarter to *four!*" he groaned. "What the dickens...?" Then he remembered!

With a sudden burst of energy, he swept back his duvet, sprung out of bed and darted along the landing in his striped pyjamas. He quickly peeped into Jamie's bedroom to see if he was back from the forest, and then pelted downstairs to the kitchen. In record time he'd poured himself a bowl of *Frosties*, doused them with milk from the fridge, grabbed a spoon from the dresser, shot into the living room and collapsed into his favourite armchair. He pressed the button on the remote control and the television under the window flickered into life.

"This is *BBC 1*. We now go over live to Stonehenge in Wiltshire for a 'television first'!" said the announcer. "We join viewers world-wide for the sunrise on Midsummer's Day...the *Summer Solstice!*"

Mr Dawson quickly pressed another button on the remote to record the programme on the video, imagining his two children curled up asleep at *Old Soulsyke!*

"Hello, you early-birds!" beamed the young lady presenter, surrounded by a crowd of excited spectators in the half-light. "Thankfully, it's a beautiful morning here with hardly a cloud in the sky! The sun's due to pop over the horizon in about ten minutes!"

Pictures of the tall, dark standing stones amid a sea of thousands of sight-seers filled the screen. Then other shots flashed by of

 blazing camp-fires...fields full of parked cars and camper-vans...a whole line of temporary toilet cabins, hot-dog stands and laughing people dancing and strumming guitars. Processions of serious bearded men in long, white, hooded cloaks...*Druids*...wound their way through the crowds. Television cameras mounted at the top of tall cranes provided aerial shots of the hordes of visitors crammed around the ancient monument. Mr Dawson stared intently at his television screen, tucking into his *Frosties*, promising himself that one day he would make the journey down to the Salisbury Plain with Jessica and Jamie and witness the event first-hand.

"It's incredible to think that viewers are watching these pictures in Australia where it's already the middle of the afternoon and in Canada where it's not even midnight yet! It's still the day before!" gushed the presenter excitedly. "Madam, where are *you* from?"

A large lady, her large husband and their two large offspring graced the screen, all dressed in gaudy checked shirts and jeans.

"Oh, my! We're from Orlando, Florida in the *U.S. of A!*" gasped the chubby face in a broad American accent. A matching chubby hand hovered just below her several chins. It was clutching a half eaten hot-dog, dripping with ketchup. "We're having such a ball over here in the Old Country! This beats *Disneyland*, anytime! Yeah, kids?"

 The two bloated children came into shot...a boy and a girl...both with their jaws wrapped around triple, mega-sized cheese, beef and bacon burgers oozing with mayo, mustard and more ketchup! Their faces looked puzzled, as if their mother had

taken leave of her senses. After all, they had seen a blazing, tropical sun nearly every day of their lives!

"Yeah, mom!" they spluttered. "If *you* say so!"

Then a thin, hollow cheeked young man wearing a flowery shirt nudged his beaming, unshaven face into the picture. He was sporting a lengthy, drooping moustache beneath a mass of brown hair...a guitar slung over his shoulder.

"Hi, there, folks!" he mumbled in some kind of English accent, waving a small yellow flag with the word '*PEACE*' written in red letters.

"And where are you from, sir?" asked the young lady presenter.

"I be from deepest Zomerzet!" the man replied.

"Have you been here for the Solstice before?"

"Oh, aar! I been comin' ere sin' I woz knee 'igh to a grazzhopper!"

The bustling crowd behind him cheered and waved cans of beer and garlands of flowers.

"Two minutes to go!" enthused the presenter, glancing over the flat fields to the distant horizon.

A hush began to descend on the vast crowd.

People stopped dancing and singing. Everyone turned their faces to the east, where an orange glow crept slowly across the sky, like spilled watercolour soaking across white tissue.

The great slabs of stone arranged in their circle thousands of years ago by ancient tribes stood proud amid a sea of present day humans.

The sun was about to peek above the horizon and send the first brilliant beams of light into the nest of standing and fallen stones.

The crowd fell silent.

You could almost touch the expectant anticipation.

The whole world was watching.

Mr Dawson stared unblinkingly at his television.

And then...

it happened!!

Chapter 18

At the very same moment as the sky flushed with brilliant sunlight and the day had broken...at the very instant the dazzling rim of the Sun nudged over the horizon...the assembled crowd gasped! Something totally unexpected had appeared in the sky!
Directly above Stonehenge!
As if it had waited for the very second the dawn cracked!

Sunlit faces were averted from the view they had all come to witness and, instead, puzzled and frightened eyes gazed upwards. Television cameras pointed into the heavens...and the whole world saw the menace that had suddenly formed above Salisbury Plain.
Jaws fell open throughout the world.
The bloated kids from Florida stopped munching.
Wow, this was even better than *Disneyland*!!
The man from Somerset had seen nothing like it in his life!
Mr Dawson at *Deer Leap* stared at his television in complete disbelief, a spoonful of *Frosties* hovering in front of his astonished face, his mouth wide open!

A great circle...a vast halo of deep purple, swirling mist hung above the entire crowd and the fields of parked cars. It was like an enormous smoke ring, but alive with glistening, churning swathes of crystals and speckled with hundreds of spots of orange and red.

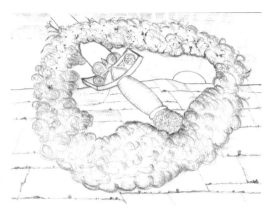

And then...a silver and gold shape began to form across the ring, stretching from side to side, as if held aloft by the mist itself. Clearer and clearer the shape became, until its full magnificence could be seen by all!

It was a dagger...its handle and hilt encrusted with dazzling, giant blue sapphires...its wide golden blade glinting in the ever brightening sunlight.

The humble, belittled crowd of human beings below stared upwards at the awesome sight. Each and every one of them knew that if the dagger was to plunge from the halo's grip it would crush hundreds of them to death. But they were held there by its power. They couldn't move. There was no panic, no mad rush to escape. No chaos. It was if they were held motionless by some mysterious hypnotic force. Some even thought it was some sort of laser-show put on by the organisers. Perhaps the ring of purple mist and the huge dagger weren't really there at all! It was all a wonderful trick of the light and electronic wizardry!

But they were wrong...very wrong!

This was the *Shym-ryn*...the gathered *Shym-ryn* from woodlands all over England. They had coalesced...united as one great, unstoppable power...and they were showing off their valuable trophy, the one that meant, at long last, that Evil Magic would prevail over Good.

None of this, of course, was known by the mere humans below. Humans were not of the magic world and had no knowledge of the forces of sorcery that existed.

But here, at Stonehenge, the cauldron of all magic, on Midsummer's Day...the normally invisible and secretive had become strikingly visible...

And, as if to show their evil intent, the *Shym-ryn* began to laugh in a mocking, scoffing, derisory tone.

The sky was filled with the sound of cackling laughter.

Louder and louder!

It became so loud, the people below had to put their hands to their ears.

Children started crying.

Adults looked at one another with a growing fear.

Then, the great circle of mist began to rotate, and with it, the giant dagger.

Slowly at first, and then faster and faster!

A wind began to blow. A cold wind, fingering the quivering humans below.

Its force became stronger and stronger until it grasped its victims and made them cling to one another and to the very stones of Stonehenge itself.

Then, huge, arching solid streaks of white crystal scored the air above the crowd, almost encasing them in some kind of gigantic, towering cage with thick bars of glistening glass. The whole of Stonehenge was enclosed.

People, at last, began to run from the standing and fallen stones of the ancient monument...but they got nowhere!

The bars of the crystal cage were impenetrable!

An invisible, glassy barrier had formed between the crystal bars!

The first to reach it scrabbled desperately at the transparent walls.

There was no escape!

And within the cage, the cackling laughter became louder and louder and the wind whirled faster and faster...

People began to panic.

Chaos began to reign supreme.

The helpless human victims were trapped in a savage maelstrom within a gigantic crystal mixing bowl crowned by a crazy, cackling revolving wheel of purple *Shym-ryn* holding on to their huge, spinning dagger. Then, even worse...tents, burning wood from camp fires, pots and pans began to be picked up and added to the danger. Flames and sparks swirled amid the confusion. The fat Americans held onto one another and the man from Somerset tried to comfort them.

Television cameras were torn from their gantries.

Screens went blank all over the world.

The planet held its breath.

Less than a minute later, pictures flickered back onto the television sets of every continent. Cameras beyond the terrified crowd sprung into action...and what they saw, and what the world saw was remarkable, if not miraculous!

Suddenly...two figures had appeared out of nowhere and were standing side by side upon the highest stone at Stonehenge...a vast slab that lay horizontally like a bridge across the top of two vertical stones.

Both were dressed in long cloaks that billowed wildly in the whirlwind that whipped around them. They battled against the gale to stay upright and slowly raised their arms, as if in defiance of the *Shym-ryns'* sorcery.

Then, when their arms were fully extended, they seemed to bellow unheard words at the purple, spinning mist way above them.

Magical words...the words of the ancient and most powerful *'StoneSpell'*!

Uttered by one wizard alone, the spell was almost supreme against all others, but when conjured by *two* magicians in unison,

it was absolutely invincible!

Merlyn and Lucius were now *united*!

Any Evil would be destroyed...instantly!

At once, the wind eased and the giant spinning dagger slowed, along with the great rotating ring of purple mist.

Suddenly, from the raised arms of the magicians, four streams of jagged fiery light shot across the sky into the mist, like bolts of lightning.

Above the astonished eyes of the crowd and before the television viewers of the world, the *Shym-ryn* began to break up and dissolve.

Verax, the dagger, began to shrink. It fell from the sky, becoming smaller and smaller. A moment later, Merlyn plucked it from the air. At last it was safely back in his hands. Without it, the *Shym-ryn* were nothing...almost powerless. Evil had been defeated! But then, the most incredible spectacle occurred!

As though to show their magical strength to the remaining, hovering *Shym-ryn*...amid more flashes of lightning...the standing and fallen stones of Stonehenge began to grow!! They swelled before the eyes of the world, bursting their way through the bars of the crystal cage, shattering the glassy barriers so the people were free. Crystal fragments flew everywhere and rained down on the ground. The fat Americans, the man from Somerset...everyone...

gathered as many as they could to keep as souvenirs! It certainly was a dawn they would never forget!

Meanwhile, Merlyn and Lucius rode their stone as it soared into the morning sky...way, way above the awe-struck crowd!

On and on, every single gigantic stone was thrusting upwards and sideways...becoming larger...and larger...and...

...until, suddenly, in the blink of an eye...

...they all *vanished* into thin air!

Stonehenge had disappeared!

Just like that!

Gone!

Chapter 19

Meanwhile, the giant strides of *Dodo* carried the Aqua Crystans and Jessica and Jamie over the desolate Yorkshire Moors as the day broke. The Sun was rising slowly into a perfectly blue sky. Safely cupped in the Gargoyle's stony clawed hands, they gazed through gaps between his fingers as the countryside rushed by.

Soon, the darkness of the night had completely dissolved and it became clear where *Dodo* was heading. He had reached the main road over the rolling heather lands and was following it towards the *Hole of Horcum*...the great depression in the landscape Jessica and Jamie had visited with their father the day before.

At that time in the morning there was hardly any traffic, just a couple of vans and a car. Fortunately, *Dodo* spotted them all well in the distance and managed to hide behind gorse bushes and even beneath a bridge over a stream. His tiny passengers dreaded to think what would have happened if the drivers had seen the strange, monstrous figure out for an early morning jog! They would probably have driven off the road in shock!

Minutes later, *Dodo* climbed a steep, bendy incline which lead to the car-park that overlooked the huge basin carved out by ice and water. Nestled in the corner of the car-park was a solitary white camper-van  with its curtains closed...its touring inhabitants, no doubt, still asleep. Quietly, the Gargoyle sat down on the rim of the great hollow and rested his weary legs. It had been a long, arduous run from Midge Hall, and there were still several miles of moorland and forest between the *Hole of Horcum* and *Aqua Crysta.*

Gently, he lowered his hands and allowed his precious passengers to stretch their legs on the short, sheep-nibbled grass. He glanced anxiously at the camper-van to make sure there were no signs of activity. Everything was peaceful and quiet. Just the sounds of warbling curlews, shrill skylarks and bleating sheep could be heard silhouetted against the silence.

The rest of the World, meanwhile, had been turned into a state of utter frenzy and bewilderment! Television and radio news stations around the planet were beaming pictures and words into the homes of astounded viewers and listeners as they woke up, went to work or ate their suppers. Traffic, factories and schools ground to a halt on every continent as people pondered on the impossible!

How *could* one of the ancient, treasured icons of Mankind simply disappear into thin air?

At the Stonehenge site itself, all the visitors silently gawped into the void once occupied by the famous circle of standing stones. Some of them even crept tentatively forward with their arms outstretched, feeling for the stones. Many headed for their cars to make a quick get-away, having decided that strange forces were at work! If

they hung around, would they vanish too?
Or was this the beginning of an alien invasion? Were some undetected extra-terrestrials hovering above England in invisible spaceships demonstrating their powers?
Nobody had an answer!
"It'll be some kind of stunt!" whispered the fat American woman to her husband. "It's amazing what they can do with laser beams now-a-days!"
"We gotta come again next year!" pleaded her son, just about to resume the demolition of his burger. "This *definitely* beats *Disneyland* and the *Space Centre* put together!"

Back at the *Hole of Horcum* car-park, the camper-van curtain twitched and the side door slowly opened. An elderly, bearded man emerged in his checked pyjamas, yawning and stretching, as he stepped down onto the tarmac. He was followed by a plumpish lady in a flowery dressing-gown with her white hair full of pink, plastic curlers.
"What a beautiful morning, Mavis!" said the man. "Today's goin' to be a right boiler! We'll be needin' the suncream for certain! How's about a cup of...?"
It was then that he spotted the strange, giant Gargoyle sitting on the edge of the road, peacefully staring out over the vast depression in the moorland.
"What the heck's *that*?" he uttered.
"What's *what*, Fred?" mumbled Mavis, squinting in the bright sunshine.
"*That!*" Fred exclaimed, pointing with a shaky arm and struggling to slip on his spectacles.
With the sudden din, *Dodo* immediately turned and eyed the unwelcome spectators. He jumped to his feet, let out a gush of his clicketty language and angrily flailed his huge, stony arms!
Mavis and Fred, open-mouthed, stared back in disbelief!
Then, in a manic blur of checked pyjamas, flowery dressing-gown and pink curlers, the panic-stricken couple scrambled back into their camper-van, slammed the door and peeped through the curtains.

What they saw next made them wish they'd stayed at home!

Suddenly, two more figures appeared...completely out of the blue...and stood one on each side of the Gargoyle. They were both dressed in long cloaks. *Dodo* became calm and turned his head to look over the great basin before him. Indeed, all three gazed into the landscape, as though they were expecting something to happen...

And, then...it *did*!!

Amazingly, and miraculously...the *Hole of Horcum* was instantly filled with vast, towering pillars of stone...stretching way, way up into the cloudless sky...each higher and wider than the tallest skyscraper!...some pairs joined at the top with gigantic stone bridges!
The thickness of the stones was immense, their height Gargantuan!
They dwarfed the whole landscape. Fields, hedges, walls, the farmhouse, and the road all became tiny...minuscule in comparison!
It was as though some giant had dumped his building bricks on the ground!
Everything had changed in the blink of an eye!
The Yorkshire Moors would never be the same again!
England would never be the same again!
Stonehenge had been moved!
And not only moved, but its new size and majestic, overwhelming presence would be gazed upon by humanity for generations to come.
In the months and years ahead, people would just stand and stare, mesmerised by the sheer magnificence!
They would fly in helicopters and hot-air balloons between the vast blocks of stone!
On some days, lofty clouds would shroud and hide the summits from view, and it would seem as though the sky itself was resting on pillars of rock. On other days, the Sun would cast the longest shadows across the purple heather. In winter, blizzard snow would coat the stones with pure

white and they would glisten with ice.

Above all, the New Stonehenge would become the most visited place on Earth! People from all over the planet...from all countries, races and religions...would come together to simply wonder and marvel!

Indeed, a spectacular, World shattering feat of magic had taken place...beyond all the understanding of mere men.

The '*StoneSpell*' had triumphed.

The power of Good over Evil had been shown.

Merlyn and Lucius, together, had been victorious.

They looked upon their work and smiled.

Even Fred and Mavis ventured back down their camper-van steps and gazed in disbelief at what towered before them.

They knew that, within the hour, the World's television and newspapers would be arriving. Stonehenge had been located, safe and sound, although somewhat larger, in the middle of the Yorkshire Moors! The question was...should they quietly get back in the camper-van and drive away, or should they stay and become the celebrated 'eye-witnesses', their faces beamed throughout the World? The fame and the fortune!

It didn't take them long to come up with an answer!

Fred put the kettle on and Mavis began to take down her curlers!

They had already forgotten about the three peculiar strangers that had appeared across the road just minutes before.

Merlyn had seen to that!

In fact, he, Lucius, *Dodo* and his precious passengers had already been whisked away in one final spell...mostly to *Aqua*

Crysta...to a joyous and wonderful reception in the *Meeting Hall Cavern*, where their sudden appearance interrupted yet another cricket match!

But what of Jessica and Jamie?

Well, they found themselves back to their full, Upper World size... riding through the forest on the backs of the young deer, *Chandar* and *Strike*!

They would be back at *Deer Leap* in next to no time!

As they sped past the ruins of *Old Soulsyke*, the tumbledown barn and the quarry, the Sun was already above the trees and the air was warm.

Pictures of their fabulous adventure were buzzing through their minds, especially the fantastic spectacle at the *Hole of Horcum*, which they'd seen from the depths of a patch of clover!

"Can't wait to see Dad!" beamed Jessica, hanging on to the albino *Chandar* as well as she could.

"Hope he remembered to video *'Sunrise at Stonehenge'*!" burst Jamie. "And you know what? We haven't hidden any treasure for his 'Treasure Hunt'!"

"I think he'll have forgotten all about that!" laughed Jessica. "He'll have been glued to the telly all morning! He may even know by now that Stonehenge has shifted north a few hundred miles!!"

On and on the young deer cantered through the glades of larch and spruce until, at last, the children reached the green track that lead out of the trees and up to *Deer Leap*.

Suddenly, just as they emerged into the bright sunlight, the deer stopped. Jessica and Jamie looked along the track.

A cool breeze swished around their bodies, making them shiver.

A purple mist swirled above them, with a hint of distant, cackling laughter coming from the tree-tops.

Then...their blood ran cold in their veins, their hearts sank...

and looks of horror crossed their faces...

...*Deer Leap* had vanished!!

Chapter 20

Heartbroken, and with tears streaming down their faces, Jessica and Jamie ran towards the place where their cottage should have stood.

"Dad! Where are you? Where are you?" screamed Jessica hysterically, rushing wildly around the remaining foundations of their beautiful home.

But her calling was in vain.

Everything had gone!

Every single trace of *Deer Leap* had disappeared as though it had never been built. Even the garden, the lawn, the fences, the shed, the Land Rover, the hutches and cages in which Jessica kept her rescued animals...!

Everything!

All that could be seen was a small pyramid of white crystals stood gleaming in the middle of the desolation, like a glassy mole-hill. It was sitting there amid the devastation, as though mocking the two children.

"It's the surviving *Shym-ryn*!" said Jamie angrily. "It's revenge for our

part in their defeat! They've
magicked *Deer Leap* away!!"
"And dad with it!!" sobbed Jessica.
"What are we going to do?"
Jamie put an arm around his sister
and tried to console her.
"We both know the power of the
magic!" he whispered gently, looking beyond the tree-tops with tear
filled eyes.
"Somewhere...somewhere out there...is dad...sitting in *Deer Leap's*
living-room...probably watching the telly, munching his *Frosties*!"
Jessica managed the smallest of smiles.
"You mean, he's lost somewhere in the magic!" she sobbed.
Jamie nodded, wiping away tears from his cheek.
"And, there's no doubt about it, sis...that one day...we'll see *him*
and *Deer Leap* again!"
        At that moment, before their eyes, the crystal pyramid
began to slowly dissolve. As it melted away, the children noticed that
there was something hidden inside the glistening, shrinking mound.
Two small, circular objects, one bigger than the other.
They were both golden, and seemed to have a spiral pattern carved into
them.
Jamie walked gingerly towards them and crouched down to get a closer
look.
"Be careful!" whispered Jessica anxiously. "They could be dangerous...
part of the *Shym-ryn's* sorcery! I don't want to lose you, too!"
"They're like those curly fossils we've seen in shops in Whitby!" said
Jamie curiously.
"You mean ammonites!"
said Jessica, still
tearfully.
"But these are
golden...and...*yes*!"

155

exclaimed Jamie. "There are *letters of the alphabet* and *numbers* carved into the spirals!"

Jamie slowly reached down to pick one up.

His fingertips moved cautiously and nervously towards the gleaming gold.

"Jamie, don't! Please don't!" burst Jessica.

But by now, Jamie's fingers were in charge. He couldn't have stopped them even if he'd wanted to.

Closer and closer they crept.

Jessica looked through moist eyes at what was happening just inches away.

"No!" she yelled, in one last attempt to stop her brother. "No, Jamie! No! No!"

At that moment, Jamie's finger touched the larger ammonite.

Instantly he felt a sharp tingle run through his hand and up his arm.

Suddenly he knew what he and Jessica must do. He smiled and looked into his sister's eyes.

Confidently, he picked up the golden ammonite and handed it to Jessica.

Still uncertain, she touched it nervously. Then she felt the same tingle,

like nettle stings darting up her arms. She had felt the same sensation before but couldn't think where.

The two children fell silent for a moment and gazed around them.

Then Jessica spoke.

"We have to go and live in *Aqua Crysta!*" she said boldly. "There is nothing for us here. Queen Venetia, Lepho, Lucius and Merlyn will help us find *Deer Leap* and dad! *Aqua Crysta* is where we need to be!"

And with that, each of them holding a golden ammonite, they

wandered back down the green track
to the quietly grazing deer. Moments
later, *Chandar* and *Strike* were
darting across the forest called
George, heading for a special place
beyond *Old Soulsyke*.

Jessica and Jamie,
both of them filled at the same time
with sadness and hope, would soon
be sitting at the top of the well,
ready to climb down into a new
and magical life. They were
certain that the tragedy they had
suffered in the Upper World
would be put right by the magic
of *Aqua Crysta*...and that,
somehow, the answer was in the
golden spirals!
Whatever it took, they *would*
find *Deer Leap* and their father!
They were sure of that!

But if only they had known what was yet to come!!

a letter from Jessica

Hello!

    Well, I never thought that I'd be writing to you from Aqua Crysta! But here I am sitting on the rocky ledge outside our house in Pillo - just two doors away from Jonathan and Jane! The view of the Pillo Falls is terrific. At the moment the flow of water is just a trickle, but soon the roar will begin as the River Floss changes direction. As you can imagine we've both got mixed feelings about being here. We were both devastated about dad and Deer Leap vanishing but everyone here keeps telling us that he's safe and sound...just kind of 'lost in the magic'! Somehow we've got to work out what to do .   I'm sure it's something to do with the letters on the golden ammonites! Have you any idea what they mean? Is there a hidden message in them, or perhaps a secret code. Let us know if you can work anything out!

    Meanwhile, I've got to say that it's brilliant down here. Our house is small but very crystally inside! All white and pink with great, long jay feathers creeping up the walls and along the ceiling. There's loads of crystal things , all made by George Chubb ...and clothes and furniture...and food. Everyone has been so kind. Lucius and Grizelda have married after being apart for so long. They also live in Pillo and let us ride Gabrielle, the horse, whenever we want!

Dodo, who had been very anxious about living in Aqua Crysta because of his appearance, is getting along fine with everyone. He lives in Pillo as well, down by the harbour. He's helping out at one of the cafes so people can get to know him.

It's been fantastic having Jonathan and Jane so close at last. They've shown us around Pillo and taken us to Middle Floss and Galdo on the 'Goldcrest'. The best thing we've done so far was the ride on 'Lightning', the rope slide that links Middle Floss, perched high up in the Cavern, down to the banks of the Floss river. It's brilliant, and so fast! I screamed all the way down! Jamie, of course, insisted on having two rides!

By the way, 'Rudolph', 'Sabre' and the rest of the giant crystalids are fine. We've visited them twice. They live in the Meeting Hall Cavern.

We're going to see the premiere of a new show there soon. It's called 'In Depths So Deep'. The Queen has invited us as 'Guests of Honour'!

Anyway, time to say goodbye. I'd love to hear from you if you want to write, especially if you can spot anything in the golden ammonites.

Keeping my fingers crossed that we find dad and Deer Leap, bye for now,

love Jessica

a letter from Jamie

Hi, everyone!

Greetings from AC! I'm writing this letter while sailing down the Floss in the 'Goldcrest' with Jonathan. We've just been playing cricket in the picnic park on the Island of Galdo. They've made a new pitch in between the everlasting toadstools. A lot of folk are learning to play and it's been great fun showing them. By the way, the hat and ball from my 'hat-trick' are next to my new bed!

It's been fantastic having Jonathan and Jane as best friends. They've taken my sis and me everywhere to show us the ropes down here! Talking of ropes you should have seen me on 'Lightning' at Middle Floss- it's a dead ace ride! I must have hit a 100 miles an hour on my second go!

Of course we're both missing dad and Deer Leap, but I'm sure we'll see them again soon! It's just a case of getting into the magic! They're lost in it somehow! Like Jess, I think the answer is in the golden ammonites. Let me know if you can work anything out. By the way, the ammonites are safely hidden in our cool new house in Pillo. It's really ace but I'm missing my models and my electric cars and...no, I've got to stop thinking about all that or I get sad. Instead, I'll think about the fact that there's no school down here and the grub is out of this world! Just try the toadstool roast with fried heather tips at the Magpie Inn in Pillo! Deee-licious!

The best place I've discovered so far is the 'Ogwood's Flying Machine Memorial Park' in Pillo. It has a

brilliant model of this super flying helicopter-like machine
that crashed many harvests ago. This guy, Ogwood, was
trying to fly up into the dizzy heights of the Cavern! But
things went wrong and he plunged into the Floss! Talking
of flying, remember the crystalids? Well, they're fine and
living in the Meeting Hall Cavern. Soon they are going to be
another form of transport down here in AC. Flying up and
down the Cavern will be ace! Although I must say it'll be
hard to beat the 'Goldcrest'! We're heading towards Pillo
at the moment. The Cave of Torrents has just flown by!

       The next time I visit Galdo, I've been invited
up to the Heights by George Chubb and Lepho to learn how
to play 'Sanctum', the board-game. I'd like to be a Grand
Master one day! I'm already getting better at
'Quintz'. Jess and I play Jonathan and Jane quite often.
There's also the next cricket match to look forward to, and
the premiere of a new show at the Meeting Hall Cavern.
Hope the crystalids don't get in the way!

       Anyway, I can just see Pillo in the distance.
I'd better stop writing.
Hope Lepho and Lucius can work out soon what to do about
the magic that's captured dad and Deer Leap.
Hope it's got nothing to do with the terrifying Shym-ryn!
Write soon,

      See you,

         Jamie

FALLING FOSS WATERFALL WOODLAND WALK
— 2 miles —

From the <u>Falling Foss Car-Park</u> (7mls. from Whitby), follow the rough track downhill from the entrance - over a stone bridge & uphill to a right turn.

A narrow, winding woodland path leads down to a small clearing in the valley with two wooden bridges.

Take the second bridge (where J&J found a clue) and climb out of the valley through tall beech trees.

(in May & June, take the first bridge and explore a beautiful bluebell wood)

Arrive at 'The Hermitage' and turn right onto the 'Coast-to-Coast' long distance path (180mls. from Robin Hood's Bay to St Bee's in Cumbria).

Just before the car-park, bear right at a 'C-to-C' sign along a path that overlooks the valley & drops down to 'Midge Hall' and 'Falling Foss' waterfall.

Finally, cross the wooden bridge, turn left over the stone bridge & climb up to the car-park.

Hope you enjoyed the walk!

(If you have the energy, the walk can be extended to May Beck & back on a 2ml. circular path!)

Watch our website
aquacrysta.com
for the 2008 publication date of
Aqua Crysta
- Part 5 -

'The Ammonite Seekers'

Now living in Aqua Crysta, follow Jessica and Jamie in another magical adventure as they crack the ammonite code and begin the quest to find 'Deer Leap' and their father in the fearsome, darkest depths beneath Whitby, both past and present!!!

Coming Soon!!
to be published in 2007

Squibbitz - 1

by James David
It's just before Christmas and ten year old Maxwell is about to start attending his 13th school, Chestnut Hill, run by headmonster, Grimmage and school-cook, Grubbage! Maxwell gets on with his class teacher Miss Teezil and falls for school heroine, Roberta. Together they take on Grimmage and Grubbage and discover their amazing secret hidden beneath the school floorboards!
Meet Maxwell, Robbie, their dance crazy single parents plus the weird staff of Chestnut Hill in this comic story by the author of the successful 'Aqua Crysta' Series.

Moonbeam Publishing

164